THE GATEWAY TRIP

TALES AND VIGNETTES OF THE HEECHEE

THE GATEWAY TRIP

TALES AND VIGNETTES
OF THE HEECHEE

FREDERIK POHL

ILLUSTRATED BY
FRANK KELLY FREAS

A DEL REY BOOK
BALLANTINE BOOKS · NEW YORK

A Del Rey Book
Published by Ballantine Books

Copyright © 1990 by Frederik Pohl
Illustrations Copyright © 1990 by Frank Kelly Freas

Library of Congress Cataloging-in-Publication Data
Pohl, Frederik.
The gateway trip : tales and vignettes of the Heechee / Frederik Pohl ; illustrated by Frank Kelly Freas.—1st ed.
p. cm.
"A Del Rey book."
ISBN 0-345-36301-9
I. Freas, Kelly. II. Title.
PS3566.036G38 1990
813′ .54—dc20
90-555
CIP

Text design by Holly Johnson
Manufactured in the United States of America

BOMC offers recordings and compact discs, cassettes and records. For information and catalog write to BOMR, Camp Hill, PA 17012.

CONTENTS

THE GATEWAY TRIP

TALES AND VIGNETTES OF THE HEECHEE

PART ONE

THE
VISIT

There was a time, half a million years ago or so, when some new neighbors came into the vicinity of the Earth's solar system. They were eager to be friendly—that is, that was what they wanted to be, if they could find anyone around to be friends with. So one day they dropped in on the third planet of the system, the one we now know as Earth itself, to see who might be at home.

It wasn't a good time to pay a call. Oh, there was plenty of *life* on Earth, no doubt of that. The planet crawled with the stuff. There were cave bears and saber-tooth cats and things like elephants and things like deer. There were snakes and fish and birds and crocodiles; and there were disease germs and scavengers; and there were forests and savannahs and vegetation of all kinds. But one element was conspicuously missing in the catalogue of terrestrial living creatures. That was a great pity, because that was the one quality the visitors were most anxious to find.

What those visitors from space couldn't find anywhere on the planet was *intelligence*. It just hadn't been invented yet.

The visitors sought it very diligently. The closest they could

3

find to a being with what they were after was a furry little creature without language, fire, or social institutions—but which did, at least, have a few promising skills. (For instance, it could manage to crunch tools out of random bits of rock.) When modern humans came along and began tracing their evolutionary roots they would name this particular brand of prehuman *"Australopithecus."* The visitors didn't call it anything in particular ... except one more disappointment in their quest for civilized company in space.

The little animals weren't very tall—about the size of a modern six-year-old—but the visitors didn't hold that against them. They had no modern humans to compare the little guys with, and anyway they weren't terribly tall themselves.

This was the chancy Pleistocene, the time when the ice was growing and retreating in Europe and North America, when African rainfall patterns swelled and diminished, and adaptability was the key for any species that wanted to stay alive. At the time the visitors arrived, the countryside in which they found a tribe of their little pets was rolling, arid savannah, covered with grasses and occasional wildflowers. Where the australopithecines had camped was in a meadow by the banks of a slow, trickly little stream that flowed into a huge salty lake a few kilometers away. On the western horizon a line of mountains stretched away out of sight. The nearest of them steamed gently. The mountains were all volcanoes, though of course the australopithecines did not have any idea what a volcano was. They did have fire, to be sure; they'd gotten that far in technological sophistication. At least, most of the time they did, when lightning started grass burning (or even when hot ash from an eruption kindled something near them, though fortunately for the peace of mind of the little people that didn't happen often). They didn't use fire for much. They had not yet considered the possibility of cooking with it, for instance. What they found it good for was keeping large nocturnal predators away, at which it sometimes succeeded.

By day they could take pretty good care of themselves. They carried stone "hand axes"—not very elaborate, just rocks chipped into more or less the shape of a fat, sharp-edged clam—and clubs that were even less impressive looking: just the unmodified long leg bones of the deerlike grazers they liked to eat. That sort of weapon would never stop a saber-tooth. But enough of them, wielded by enough of the screaming little ape-men, could usually deter the hyenas that were the savannah's fiercest predators, especially if the little folk had first discouraged the hyena pack by pelting it with

rocks from a distance. They didn't usually succeed in killing the hyenas, but most of the time they did convince the animals that their time would be better spent on more defenseless prey.

The little people did lose a baby to a carnivore now and then, of course, or an old person whose worn-out teeth were making his or her life chancy anyway. They could stand that. They seldom lost anyone important to the well-being of the tribe—except when hunting, of course. But they didn't have any choice about taking the risks of the hunt. They had to hunt to eat.

Although the australopithecines were tiny, they were quite strong. They tended to have pot bellies, but the gluteus maximus was quite small—even the females had no hips to speak of. Their faces were not very human: no chin worth mentioning, a broad nose, tiny ears almost hidden in the head fur—you wouldn't call it hair yet. An average australopithecine's skull did not have room for any large supply of brains. If you poured the brains out of his sloped skull into a pint beer mug, they would probably spill over the edge, but not much.

Of course, no modern beer drinker would do that, but one of the little furry people might have—gladly. In their diet, brains were a delicacy. Even each other's.

The visitors didn't think much of the furry people's eating habits. Still, the creatures had one anatomical characteristic that interested the visitors a lot—in a sort of winky-jokey way, with sexual overtones. Like the visitors, the australopithecines were bipeds. Unlike the visitors, their legs were positioned so close to each other that they actually rubbed together at the thighs when they walked—and for the males, at least, that seemed to the visitors to present real problems, since the male sexual organs hung between the thighs.

(Some hundreds of thousands of years later, the then paramount denizens of Earth, the human race, would ask themselves similar questions about the long-gone visitors . . . and they, too, would fail to understand.)

So the visitors from space looked the little furry creatures over for a while, then chirruped their disappointment to each other, got back in their spaceships, and went glumly away.

Their visit had not been a total loss. Any planet that bore life at all was a rare jewel in the galaxy. Still, they had really been hoping for a more sophisticated kind of life—someone to meet and be friends and interchange views and have discussions with. These little furry animals definitely weren't up to any of that. The visitors didn't leave them quite untouched, though. The visitors had learned, from dismal experience, that faintly promising species of creatures might easily die off, or take a wrong turning somewhere along the evolutionary line, and so never realize their promise. So the visitors had a policy of establishing a sort of, well, call them "game preserves." Accordingly, they took a few of the australopithecines away with them in their spaceships when they left. They put the little beasts in a safe place, in the hope that they might amount to something after all. Then the visitors departed.

Time passed . . . a lot of time.

The australopithecines never did get very far on Earth. But then their close relatives—the genus *Homo*, better known as you and me and all our friends—came along. The genus *Homo* people worked out a lot better. Over some five hundred thousand years, in fact, they did just about all the things the visitors had hoped for from the australopithecines.

These "humans," as they called themselves, were pretty clever at thinking things up. As the ages passed they invented a lot of neat stuff—the wheel, and agriculture, and draft animals, and cities, and levers and sailing ships and the internal combustion engine and credit cards and radar and spacecraft. They didn't invent them all at once, of course. And not everything they invented turned out to be an absolute boon, because along the way they also invented clubs and swords and bows and catapults and cannon and nuclear missiles. These humans had a real talent for messing things up.

For instance, a lot of their inventions were the kind that looked as though they *ought* to do something, but really did something very different—which was the case with all their "peacekeeping" gadgets, none of which kept any peace. "Medicine" was another case in point. They invented what they called medicine quite early— that is, they invented the practice of doing all sorts of bizarre things to people who were unfortunate enough to get sick. Ostensibly the things they did were intended to make the sick person better; often enough they went the other way. At best, they generally didn't

help. The man who was dying of malaria may have been grateful to his local doctor for putting on the devil mask and dancing around the bed, but the patient died anyway. By the time human medicine reached the point where a sick person's chances of recovery were better with a doctor than without one—that took about 499,900 of those 500,000 years—humans had managed to find a more efficient way of screwing things up. They had invented money. Human medicine became fairly good at curing many human ailments, but more and more of the human race began to have trouble finding the money to pay for it.

And along about the same time, the humans who lived on this little green planet called Earth finally reached the point where they could get off it for the first time. The age of human exploration of space had begun.

In a sense, this was a happy coincidence. By the time human beings reached the point of being able to launch a spaceship, it may well have been true that it was also getting to be a good time to think seriously about leaving the Earth, for good. The Earth was a pretty good place to be rich in. It was a very bad one to be poor.

By then, of course, the people who had dropped in on the australopithecines were long gone.

9

In their yearning quest for some other intelligent race to talk to they had surveyed more than half the galaxy. Actually, there were some successes, or almost successes. They did find a few promising species—well, at least as promising as the poor, dumb australopithecines.

Probably the race that came closest to what they were looking for were the ones they called the Slow Swimmers. These people (no, they didn't look a bit like "people," but in fairness that was more or less what they were) lived in the dense liquid-gas atmosphere of a heavy planet. The Slow Swimmers had language, at least. In fact, they sang beautiful, endless songs in their language, which the visitors finally managed to puzzle out enough to understand. The Slow Swimmers even had cities—sort of cities—well, what they had was domiciles and public structures that floated around in the soupy mud they lived in. The Slow Swimmers weren't a lot of fun to talk to, but the main reason for that was that they were, you'd better believe it, really *slow*. If you tried to talk to them you had to wait a week for them to get out a word, a year to finish the first few bars of one of their songs—and a couple of lifetimes, anyway, to carry on a real conversation. That wasn't the Slow Swimmers' fault. They lived at such a low temperature that everything they did was orders of magnitude slower than warm-blooded oxygen-breathers like human beings—or like the visitors from space.

Then the visitors found someone else . . . and that was a whole other thing, and a very scary one.

They stopped looking after that.

When human beings went into space they had their own agenda, which wasn't quite the same as the purposes of their ancient visitors. The humans weren't really looking for other intelligences, at least not in the same way. The human telescopes and probe rockets had told them long ago that no intelligent aliens were going to be found,

at least in their own solar system—and they had little hope of going any farther than that.

The humans might well have looked for their long-ago visitors if they had had any idea they existed. But, of course, they didn't.

Maybe the best way to find another intelligent race is to be lucky rather than purposeful. When human beings got to the planet Venus it didn't look very promising. The first humans to look at it didn't "look"—no one could see very far through its miserably dense and murky air—they just circled around it in orbit, feeling for surface features with radar. What they found wasn't encouraging. Certainly when the first human rockets landed beside the Rift Valley of Aphrodite Terra and the first parties began to explore the inhospitable surface of Venus they had no hope of finding life there.

And, sure enough, they didn't. But then, in a part of Venus called Aino Planitia, a geologist made a discovery. There was a fissure—call it a tunnel, though at first they thought it might be a lava tube—under the surface of the planet. It was long, it was regular . . . and it had no business being there.

The Venusian explorers, without warning, had found the first signs of that half-million-year-ago visit . . .

PART TWO

THE MERCHANTS OF VENUS

I

My name is Audee Walthers, my job airbody driver, my home on Venus—in the Spindle or in a Heechee hut most of the time; wherever I happen to be when I feel sleepy otherwise.

Until I was twenty-five I lived on Earth, mostly in Amarillo Central. My father was deputy governor of Texas. He died when I was still in college, but he left me enough in civil-service dependency benefits for me to finish school, get a master's in business administration, and pass the journeyman's examination as clerk-typist in the Service. So I was set up for life, or so most people would have thought.

After I had tried it for a few years, I made a discovery. I didn't like the life I was set up for. It wasn't so much for the reasons anyone might expect. Amarillo Central wasn't all that bad. I don't mind having to wear a smog suit, can get along with neighbors even when there are eight thousand of them to the square mile, tolerate noise, can defend myself against the hoodlum kid gangs—no, it wasn't Texas itself that bothered me. It was what I was doing with my life in Texas, and, for that matter, what I would have to be doing with it anywhere else on Earth.

So I got out.

I sold my UOPWA journeyman's card to a woman who had to mortgage her parents' room to pay for it; I mortgaged my own pension accrual; I took the little bit of money I had saved in the bank . . . and I bought a one-way ticket to Venus.

There wasn't anything strange about that. It was what every kid tells himself he's going to do when he grows up. The difference is that I did it.

I suppose it would all have been different if I'd had any chance at Real Money. If my father had been full governor, with all those chances for payoffs and handouts, instead of being just a civil-service flunky . . . If the dependency benefits he'd left me had included unlimited Full Medical . . . If I'd been at the top of the heap instead of stuck in the oppressed middle, squeezed from both directions . . .

It didn't happen that way. So I took the pioneer route and wound up trying to make a living out of Terrestrial tourists in Venus's main place, the Spindle.

Everybody has seen pictures of the Spindle, just as with the Colosseum and Niagara Falls. The difference, of course, is that the only view you ever get of the Spindle is from inside it. It's under the surface of Venus, in a place called Alpha Regio.

Like everything worth looking at on Venus, the Spindle was something left over by the Heechee. Nobody had ever figured out exactly what it was the Heechee wanted with an underground chamber three hundred meters long and spindle-shaped, but there it was. So we used it. It was the closest thing Venus had to a Times Square or a Champs Elysées. All Terry tourists head first for the Spindle, so that's where we start fleecing them.

My own airbody-rental business is reasonably legitimate, as tourist ventures go on Venus—I mean, at least it is if you don't count the fact that there isn't really much worth seeing on Venus that wasn't left there, under the surface, by the Heechee. All the other tourist traps in the Spindle are reasonably crooked. Terries don't seem to mind that. They must know they're being taken, though. They all load up on Heechee prayer fans and doll-heads, and those paperweights of transparent plastic in which a contoured globe of Venus swims in a kind of orangy-browny snowstorm of make-believe blood-diamonds, fire-pearls, and fly ash. None of the souvenirs are worth the price of their mass charge back to Earth, but to a tourist who can get up the price of the interplanetary passage in the first place I don't suppose that matters.

To people like me, who can't get up the price of anything, the tourist traps matter a lot. We live on them.

I don't mean that we draw our excess disposable income from them. I mean that they are how we get the price of what to eat and where to sleep. If we don't have the price we die.

There aren't many legitimate ways of earning money on Venus. There's the army, if you call that legitimate; the rest is tourism and dumb luck. The dumb-lucky chances—oh, like winning a lottery, or striking it rich in the Heechee diggings, or blundering into a well-paying job with one of the scientific expeditions—are all real long shots. For our bread and butter, almost everybody on Venus depends on Terry tourists, and if we don't milk them dry when we get the chance we've had it.

Of course, there are tourists and then there are tourists. They come in three varieties. The difference between them is celestial mechanics.

Class III is the quick and dirty kind. Back on Earth, they are merely well-to-do. The Class IIIs come to Venus every twenty-six months at Hohmann-orbit time, riding the minimum-energy circuit from Earth. Because of the critical time windows of the Hohmann orbits they never can stay on Venus for more than three weeks. So they come out on their guided tours, determined to get the most out of the quarter-million-dollar minimum cabin fare their rich grandparents have given them for a graduation present, or that they've saved up for a second honeymoon, or whatever. The bad thing about them is that they don't usually have much extra money to spend, since they've spent it all on fares. The nice thing is that there are a lot of them. When the tour ships are in all the rental rooms on Venus are filled. Sometimes they'll have six couples sharing a single partitioned cubicle, two pairs at a time, hot-bedding eight-hour shifts around the clock. Then people like me hole up in Heechee huts on the surface and rent out our own below-ground rooms, and that way maybe make enough money to live a few months.

But you couldn't make enough out of Class IIIs to live until the next Hohmann-orbit time, so when the Class II tourists come in we cut each other's throats over them.

The Class IIs are the medium-rich. What you might call the poor millionaires; the ones whose annual income is in the low seven figures. They can afford to come in powered orbits, taking a hundred days or so for the run, instead of the long, slow Hohmann drift. The price for that runs a million dollars and up, so there aren't nearly as many of the Class II tourists. But there are a few trickling in every month or so at the time of reasonably favorable orbital conjunctions. They also have more money to spend when they get to Venus. So do those other Class II medium-rich ones who wait for the four or five times in a decade when the ballistics of the planets sort themselves into the low-energy configuration that allows them to hit three planets in an orbit that doesn't have much higher energy costs than the straight Earth–Venus run. They hit us first, if we're lucky, and then go on to Mars. (As if there was anything to do on Mars!) If they've gone the other way around, we get the leavings from the Martian colonists. That's bad, because the leavings are never very much.

But the very rich—ah, the very rich! The Class I marvels! They come as they like, in orbital season or not, and they can *spend*.

When my informant on the landing pad reported the *Yuri Gagarin* incoming, under private charter, my money nose began to quiver.

Whoever was on it had to be a good prospect. It was out of season for anybody except the really rich. The only question on my mind was how many of my competitors would be trying to cut my throat to get to the *Gagarin*'s passengers first . . . while I was doing my best to cut theirs.

It was important to me. I happened to have a pretty nasty cash-flow problem just then.

Airbody rental takes a lot more capital than, say, opening a prayer-fan booth. I'd been lucky in buying my airbody cheap when the fellow I worked for died. I didn't have too many competitors; a couple of the ones who might've competed were out of service for repairs, and a couple more had kited off on Heechee diggings of their own.

So, actually, I considered that I might have the *Gagarin*'s passengers, whoever they were, pretty much to myself . . . assuming they could be interested in taking a trip outside the maze of Heechee tunnels right around the Spindle.

I had to assume that they would be interested, because I needed the money very much. You see, I had this little liver condition. It was getting close to total failure. The way the doctors explained it to me, I had three choices: I could go back to Earth and live for a while on external dialysis. Or I could somehow find the money for a transplant. Or I could die.

||

The name of the fellow who had chartered the *Gagarin* turned out to be Boyce Cochenour. Age, apparently around forty. Height, easily two meters. Ancestry, Irish-American-French.

I recognized his type at once: he was the kind that's used to being the boss wherever he is. I watched him come into the Spindle, looking as though he owned it and everything it held and was thinking about liquidating his holdings. He sat down in Sub Vastra's imitation of a combination Paris boulevard–Heechee sidewalk café. "Scotch," he said, without even looking to see if he was being waited on. He was. Vastra hurried to pour John Begg over supercooled ice and hand it to him, all crackling with cold and numbing to the lips. "Smoke," he said, and the girl with him instantly lit a cigarette and passed it to him. "Crummy-looking dump," he observed, glancing around, and Vastra fell all over himself to agree.

I sat down next to them—well, I mean not at the same table; I

didn't even look their way. But from the next table I could hear everything they said. Vastra didn't look at me, either, but of course he had seen me come in and knew I had my eye on these promising new marks. I had to let his number-three wife take my order instead of Vastra himself, because Vastra certainly wasn't going to waste his time on a tunnel-rat when he had a charter-ship Terry at his table. "The usual," I said to her, meaning straight alk in a tumble of soft drink. "And a copy of your briefing," I added more softly. Her eyes twinkled understandingly at me over her flirtation veil. Cute little vixen. I patted her hand in a friendly way and left a rolled-up bill in it; then she left.

The Terry was inspecting his surroundings, which included me. I looked back at him, polite but distant, and he gave me a sort of quarter-nod and turned back to Subhash Vastra. "Since I'm here," he said, in all the right tones for a bored tourist, "I might as well sample whatever action you've got. What's to do here?"

Sub Vastra grinned widely, like a tall, skinny frog. "Ah, whatever you wish, sah! Entertainment? In our private rooms we have the finest artists of three planets, nautch dancers, music, fine comedians—"

"We've got enough of that stuff in Cincinnati. I didn't come to Venus for a nightclub act." Cochenour couldn't have known it, of course, but that was the right decision to make; Sub's private rooms were way down the list of night spots on Venus, and even the top of the list wasn't much.

"Of course, sah! Then perhaps you would like to consider a tour?"

"Aw." Cochenour shook his head. "What's the point of running around? Does any of the planet look any different than the space pad we came in on, right over our heads?"

Vastra hesitated. I could see him doing swift arithmetic in his head, measuring the chance of persuading the Terry to go for a surface tour against what he might get from me as his commission on something bigger. He didn't look my way. Honesty won out—

19

that is, honesty reinforced by a quick appraisal of Cochenour's gullibility. "Not much different, no, sah," he admitted. "All pretty hot and dry on the surface, all the same, pretty much. But I did not think of the surface."

"What then?"

"Ah, the Heechee warrens, sah! There are many miles of same just below this settlement. A reliable guide could be found—"

"Not interested," Cochenour growled. "Not in anything that close."

"Sah?"

"If a guide can lead us through them," Cochenour explained, "that means they've all been explored, which means if there was anything good in them it's been looted already. What's the fun of that?"

"Of course!" Vastra cried immediately. "I understand your meaning, sah." He looked noticeably happier, and I could feel his radar reaching out to make sure I was listening, though he still didn't look in my direction at all. "To be sure," he went on weightily, an expert explaining complexities to a valued client, "there is always the chance that one may find new digs, sah, provided one knows where to look. Am I correct in assuming that this would interest you?"

The Third of Vastra's house had brought me my drink and a thin powder-faxed slip of paper. "Thirty percent," I whispered to her. "Tell Sub. Only no bargaining and no getting anybody else to bid." She nodded and winked; she'd been listening too, of course, and she was as sure as I was that this Terry was firmly on the hook.

It had been my intention to nurse my drink as long as I could, while the mark ripened under Vastra's skillful ministrations, but it looked like prosperity was looming ahead. I was ready to celebrate. I took a long, happy swallow.

Unfortunately, the hook didn't seem to have a barb. Unaccountably, the Terry shrugged. "Waste of time, I bet," he grumbled. "I mean, really, if anybody knew where to look, why wouldn't he have looked there on his own already, right?"

"Ah, mister!" Vastra cried, beginning to panic. "But I assure you, there are hundreds of tunnels not yet explored! Thousands, sah! And in them, who knows, treasures beyond price very likely!"

Cochenour shook his head. "Let's skip it," he said. "Just bring us another drink. And see if you can't get the ice really cold this time."

That shook me. My nose for money was rarely wrong.

I put down my drink and half turned away to hide what I was doing from the Terries as I looked at the fax of Sub's briefing report on them to see if it might explain to me why Cochenour had lost interest so fast.

The report couldn't answer that question. It did tell me a lot, though. The woman with Cochenour was named Dorotha Keefer. She had been traveling with him for a couple of years now, according to their passports, though this was their first time off Earth. There was no indication of a marriage between them—or of any intention of it, at least on Cochenour's part. Keefer was in her early twenties—real age, not simulated by drugs and transplants. While Cochenour himself was well over ninety.

He did not, of course, look anywhere near that. I'd watched him walk over to their table, and he moved lightly and easily, for a big man. His money came from land and petro-foods. According to the synoptic on him, he had been one of the first oil millionaires to switch over from selling oil as fuel for cars to oil as a raw material for food production, growing algae in the crude oil that came out of his well and selling the algae, in processed form, for human consumption. So then he had stopped being a mere millionaire and turned into something much bigger.

That accounted for the way he looked. He had been living on Full Medical, with extras. The report said that his heart was titanium and plastic. His lungs had been transplanted from a twenty-year-old killed in a copter crash. His skin, muscles, and fats—not to mention his various glandular systems—were sustained by hormones and cell-builders at what had to be a cost of several thousand dollars a day.

To judge by the way he stroked the thigh of the girl next to him, he was getting his money's worth. He looked and acted no more than forty, at most—except perhaps for the look of his pale-blue, diamond-bright, weary, and disillusioned eyes.

He was, in short, a *lovely* mark.

I couldn't afford to let him get away. I swallowed the rest of the drink and nodded to the Third of Vastra for another. There had to be some way, somehow, to land him for a charter of my airbody.

All I had to do was find it.

Of course, on the other side of the little railing that set Vastra's café off from the rest of the Spindle, half the tunnel-rats on Venus were thinking the same thoughts. This was the worst of the low season. The Hohmann crowd was still three months in the future, and all of us were beginning to run low on money. My need for a liver transplant was just a little extra incentive; of the hundred maze-runners I could see out of the corner of my eye, ninety-nine needed to cut a helping out of this tourist's bankroll as much as I did, just for the sake of staying alive.

We couldn't all do it. He looked pretty fat, but nobody could have been fat enough to feed us all. Two of us, maybe three, maybe even half a dozen might score enough to make a real difference. No more than that.

I had to be one of those few.

I took a deep swallow of my second drink, tipped the Third of Vastra's House lavishly—and conspicuously—and turned idly around until I was facing the Terries.

The girl was bargaining with the knot of souvenir vendors leaning over the rail. "Boyce?" she called over her shoulder. "What's this thing for?"

He bent over the rail and peered. "Looks like a fan," he told her.

"Heechee prayer fan, right!" the dealer cried. I knew him,

Booker Allemang, an old-timer in the Spindle. "Found it myself, miss! It'll grant your every wish, letters every day from people reporting miraculous results—"

"It's sucker bait," Cochenour grumbled. "Buy it if you want to."

"But what does it do?" she asked.

Cochenour had an unpleasant laugh; he demonstrated it. "It does what any fan does. It cools you down. Not that you need that," he added meanly, and looked over to me with a grin.

My cue.

I finished my drink, nodded to him, stood up, and walked over to their table. "Welcome to Venus," I said. "May I help you?"

The girl looked at Cochenour for permission before she said, "I thought this fan thing was pretty."

"Very pretty," I agreed. "Are you familiar with the story of the Heechee?"

I looked inquiringly toward the empty chair, and, as Cochenour didn't tell me to get lost, I sat down in it and went on. "The Heechee built these tunnels a long time ago—maybe a quarter of a million years. Maybe more. They seem to have occupied them for some time, anything up to a century or two, give or take a lot. Then they went away again. They left a lot of junk behind, and some things that weren't junk. Among other things, they left thousands of these fans. Some local con-man—it wasn't BeeGee here, I think, but somebody like him—got the idea of calling the things 'prayer fans' and selling them to tourists to make wishes on."

Allemang had been hanging on my every word, trying to guess where I was going. "Partly, that's right," he admitted.

"All of it is right. But you two are too smart for that kind of thing. Still," I added, "look at the fans. They're pretty enough to be worth having even without the story."

"They are, absolutely!" Allemang cried. "See how this one sparkles, miss! And this black and gray crystal, how nice it looks with your fair hair!"

The girl unfurled the black and gray one. It came rolled like a diploma, only cone-shaped. It took just the slightest pressure of the thumb to keep it open, and it really sparkled very prettily as she gently waved it about. Like all the Heechee fans, it weighed only about ten grams, not counting the simulated-wood handles that people like BeeGee Allemang put on them. Its crystalline lattice caught the lights from the luminous Heechee-metal walls, as well as from the fluorescents and gas tubes we maze-runners had installed, and tossed all the lights back as shimmering, iridescent sparks.

"This fellow's name is Booker Garey Allemang," I told the Terries. "He'll sell you the same goods as any of the others, but he won't cheat you as much as most of them—especially with me watching."

Cochenour looked at me dourly, then beckoned Sub Vastra for another round of drinks. "All right," he said. "If we buy any of this we'll buy from you, Booker Garey Allemang. But not now." He turned to me. "And now what is it that you hope I'll buy from you?"

I spoke right up. "My airbody and me. If you want to go looking for new tunnels, we're both as good as you can get."

He didn't hesitate. "How much?"

"One million dollars," I said immediately. "Three-week charter, all found."

This time he didn't answer at once, although I was pleased to see that the price didn't seem to scare him away. He looked as receptive, or at least as merely bored, as ever. "Drink up," he said, as Vastra and his Third served us, and then he gestured with his glass to the Spindle around us. "Do you know what this is for?" he asked.

"Do you mean, why the Heechee built it? No. The Heechee weren't any taller than we are, so it wasn't this big because they needed headroom. And it was entirely empty when it was found."

He looked around, without excitement, at the busy scene. The Spindle is always busy. It had balconies cut into the sloping sides of the cavern, with eating and drinking places like Vastra's along there, and rows of souvenir booths. Most of them were of course empty, in this slow season. But there were still a couple hundred maze-rats living in and near the Spindle, and the number of them hovering around us had been quietly growing all the time Cochenour and the girl had been sitting there.

He said, "There's nothing much to see here, is there?" I didn't argue. "There's nothing but a hole in the ground, full of people trying to take my spare change away from me." I shrugged; he grinned at me—less meanly than before, I thought. "So why did I come to Venus, if that's how I feel? Well, that's a good question, but since you didn't ask it I don't have to answer."

He looked at me to see if I might be going to press the matter. I didn't.

"So let's just talk business," he went on. "You want a million dollars. Let's see what that pays for. It'd be around a hundred K to charter an airbody. A hundred and eighty K or so to rent equipment for a week, times three weeks. Food, supplies, permits, another fifty K. So we're up close to seven hundred thousand, not counting your own salary or what you have to give our host here as his cut for not throwing you off the premises. Is that about the way it adds up, Walthers?"

I had not expected him to be a cost-accountant. I had a little difficulty swallowing the drink I had been holding in my mouth, but I managed to say, "Close enough, Mr. Cochenour." I didn't see any point in telling him that I already owned the airbody, as well as most of the other needed equipment—that was the only way there was going to be anything left for me after paying off all the other charges. But I wouldn't have been surprised to find out that he knew that, too.

Then he surprised me. "Sounds like the right price," he said casually. "You've got a deal. I want to leave as soon as possible, which I want to be, um, just about this time tomorrow."

"Fair enough," I said, getting up. "I'll see you then."

I avoided Sub Vastra's thunderstricken expression as I left. I had some work to do, and a little thinking. Cochenour had caught me off base, and that's a bad place to be when you can't afford to make a mistake. I knew he hadn't missed the fact that I'd called him by name. That was all right. He would easily guess that I had checked him out immediately, and his name was the least of the things he would assume I had found out about him.

But it was a little surprising that he had known mine.

I had three major errands. The first thing I had to do was double-check my equipment to make sure it would still stand up against all the nastiness Venus can visit on a machine—or a person. The second was to go to the local union office and register a contract with Boyce Cochenour for validation, with a commission clause for Vastra.

The third was to see my doctor. The liver hadn't been giving me much trouble for a while, but then I hadn't been drinking much grain alcohol for a while.

The equipment turned out to be all right. It took me about an hour to complete the checks, but by the end of the time I was reasonably sure that I had all the gear and enough spare parts to keep us going. The Quackery was on the way to the union office, so I stopped in to see Dr. Morius first. It didn't take long. The news was no worse than I had been ready for. The doctor put all his instruments on me and studied the results carefully—about a hundred and fifty dollars worth of carefully—and then expressed the guarded hope that I would survive three weeks away from his office, provided I took all the stuff he gave me and wandered no more than usual from the diet he insisted on. "And when I get back?" I asked.

"Same as I've been telling you, Audee," he said cheerily. "You can expect total hepatic collapse in, oh, maybe ninety days." He patted his fingertips, looking at me optimistically. "I hear you've got a live one, though. Want me to make a reservation for your transplant?"

"How live did you hear my prospect was?" I asked.

He shrugged. "The price is the same in any case," he told me good-naturedly. "Two hundred K for the new liver, plus the hospital, anesthesiologist, pre-op psychiatrist, pharmaceuticals, my own fee—you've already got the figures."

I did. And I had already calculated that with what I might make from Cochenour, plus what I had put away, plus a loan on the airbody I could just about meet it. Leaving me broke when it was over, of course. But alive.

"Happens I've got one in stock now that's just your size," Dr. Morius said, half-kidding.

I didn't doubt him. There are always plenty of spare parts in the Quackery. That's because people are always getting themselves killed, one way and another, and their heirs do their best to fatten up the estate by selling off the innards. I dated one of the quacks once or twice. When we'd been drinking she took me down to the Cold Cuts department and showed me all the frozen hearts and lungs and bowels and bladders, each one already dosed with antiallergens so it wouldn't be rejected, all tagged and packed away, ready for a paying customer. It was a pity I wasn't in that class, because then Dr. Morius could have pulled one out, warmed it up in the

microwave, and slapped it in. When I joked—I told her I was jok-
ing—about swiping just one little liver for me, the date went sour,
and not long after that she packed it in and went back to Earth.

I made up my mind.

"Make the reservation," I said. "Three weeks from today." And
I left him looking mildly pleased, like a Burmese hydro-rice planter
watching the machines warm up to bring in another crop. Dear
Daddy. Why hadn't he sent me through medical school instead of
giving me an education?

It would have been nice if the Heechee had been the same size
as human beings, instead of being just that little bit shorter. It was
reflected in their tunnels. In the smaller ones, like the one that led
to the Local 88 union office, I had to half crouch all the way.

The deputy organizer was waiting for me. He had one of the
very few good jobs on Venus that didn't depend on tourism—or at
least not directly. He said, "Subhash Vastra's been on the line. He
says you agreed to thirty percent, and besides you took off without
paying your bar bill to the Third of his house."

"Admitted, both ways."

He made a note. "And you owe me a little too, Audee. Three
hundred for the powder-fax copy of my report on your pigeon. A
hundred for validating your contract with Vastra. And you're going
to need a new guide's license; sixteen hundred for that."

I gave him my currency card, and he checked the total out of
my account into the local's. Then I signed and card-stamped the
contract he'd drawn up. Vastra's thirty percent would not be on
the whole million dollars, but on my net. Even so, he was likely to
make as much out of it as I would, at least in liquid cash, because I
was going to have to pay off the outstanding balances on equipment.
The banks would carry a man until he scored, but then they wanted
to get paid in full . . . because they knew how long it might be until
he scored again.

The deputy verified the signed contract. "That's that, then. Anything else I can do for you?"

"Not at your prices," I told him.

He gave me a sharp look, with a touch of envy in it. "Ah, you're putting me on, Audee. 'Boyce Cochenour and Dorotha Keefer, traveling S.S. *Yuri Gagarin*, Odessa registry, carrying no other passengers,'" he quoted from the report he'd intercepted for us. "No other passengers! Why, you can be a rich man, Audee, if you work this customer right."

"Rich man is more than I ask," I told him. "All I want is to be a living one."

It wasn't entirely true. I did have some little hope—not much, not enough to talk about, and in fact I'd never said a word about it to anyone—that I might be coming out of this rather better than just alive.

There was, however, a problem.

The problem was that if we did find anything, Boyce Cochenour would get most of it. If a tourist like Cochenour goes on a guided hunt for new Heechee tunnels, and he happens to find something valuable—tourists have, you know; not often, but enough to keep them hopeful—then it's the charterer who gets the lion's share. Guides get a taste, but that's all. We just work for the man who pays the bills.

Of course, I could have gone out by myself at any time and prospected on my own. Then anything I found would be all mine. But in my case, that was a really bad idea. If I staked myself to a trip and lost I wouldn't just be wasting my time and fifty or a hundred K on used-up supplies and wear and tear on the airbody. If I lost, I would be dead shortly thereafter, when that beat-up old liver finally gave out.

I needed every penny Cochenour would pay me just to stay alive. Whether we struck it rich or not, my fee from him would take care of that.

Unfortunately for my peace of mind, I had a notion that I knew where something very interesting might be found; and my problem was that, as long as I had the standard charterer's-rights contract with Cochenour, I really couldn't afford to find it.

The last stop I made was in my sleeping room. Under my bed, keystoned into the rock, was a guaranteed break-proof safe that held some papers I wanted to have in my pocket from then on.

See, when I first came to Venus it wasn't scenery that interested me. I wanted to make my fortune.

I didn't see much of the surface of Venus then, or for nearly two years after that. You don't see much in the kind of spacecraft that can land you on Venus. To survive the squeeze of a ninety-thousand-millibar surface pressure means you need a hull that's a little more rugged than the bubble-ships that go to the Moon or Mars or farther out. They don't put unnecessary windows into the skin of Venus-landers. That didn't matter much, because there isn't much on the surface of Venus that you *can* see. Everything the tourists can snap pictures of is *inside* Venus, and every bit of it once belonged to the Heechee.

We don't know much about the Heechee. We don't even rightly know their name. "Heechee" isn't a name, it's how somebody once wrote down the sound that a fire-pearl makes when you stroke it. As that was the only sound anybody had ever heard that was connected with the Heechee, it got to be their name.

The "hesperologists" don't have any idea where these Heechee folks came from, although there are some markings that seem to be a star chart—pretty much unrecognizable; if we knew the exact position of every star in the galaxy a few hundred thousand years ago we might be able to locate them from that. Maybe. Assuming they came from this galaxy.

I wonder sometimes what they wanted. Escaping a dying planet? Political refugees? Tourists whose cruise ship had a breakdown between somewhere and somewhere, so that they had to hang around long enough to repair whatever they had to repair to get themselves going again? I don't know. Nobody else does, either.

But, though the Heechee packed up nearly everything when they left, leaving behind only empty tunnels and chambers, there were a few scraps here and there that either weren't worth taking or were overlooked: all those "prayer fans," enough empty containers of one kind or another to look like a picnic ground at the end of a hard summer, some trinkets and trifles. I guess the best known of the "trifles" is the anisokinetic punch, the carbon crystal that transmits a blow at a ninety-degree angle. That made somebody a few billion just by being lucky enough to find one, though not until somebody else had made his own billions by being smart enough to analyze and duplicate it. But that's the best of the lot. What we usually find is, face it, just junk. There must once have been good stuff worth a million times as much as those sweepings.

Did they take all the good stuff with them when they left?

That was another thing that nobody knew. I didn't know, either, but I did think I knew something that had a bearing on it.

I thought I knew a place where a Heechee tunnel had had something pretty neat in it, long ago; and that particular tunnel wasn't near any of the explored diggings.

I didn't kid myself. I knew that that wasn't a guarantee of anything.

But it was something to go on. Maybe when those last ships left the Heechee were getting impatient, and maybe not as thorough at cleaning up behind themselves.

And that was what being on Venus was all about.

What other possible reason was there for being there? The life of a maze-rat was marginal at best. It took fifty thousand a year to stay alive—air tax, capitation tax, water assessment, subsistence-level bill for food. If you wanted to eat meat more than once a month, or demanded a private cubicle of your own to sleep in, it cost a lot more than that.

Guide's papers cost a week's living costs. When any of us bought

31

a set of them, we were gambling that week's cost of living against the chance of a big enough strike, either from the Terry tourists or from what we might find, to make it possible to go home to Earth—where no one died for lack of air and no one was thrust out into the high-pressure incinerator that was Venus's atmosphere. Not *just* to get back to Earth, but to get back there in the style every maze-rat had set himself as a goal when he headed sunward in the first place: with money enough to live the full life of a human being on Full Medical.

That was what I wanted: the Big Score.

IV

The last thing I did that night was to visit the Hall of Discoveries. That wasn't just the whim of the moment. I'd made an arrangement with the Third of Vastra's House.

The Third winked at me over her flirtation veil and turned to her companion, who looked around and recognized me. "Hello, Mr. Walthers," she said.

"I thought I might find you here," I said, which was no more than the truth. I didn't know what to call the woman. My own mother had been old-fashioned enough to take my father's name when they married, but that didn't apply here, of course. "Miss Keefer" was accurate, "Mrs. Cochenour" might have been diplomatic; I got around the problem by saying, "Since we'll be seeing a lot of each other, how about getting right on to first names?"

"Audee, is it?"

I gave her a twelve-tooth smile. "Swede on my mother's side, old Texan on my father's. Name's been in his family a long time, I guess—Dorotha."

Vastra's Third had melted into the background; I took over, to show this Dorotha Keefer what the Hall of Discoveries was all about.

The Hall is there for the purposes of getting Terry tourists and prospectors hotted up, so they'll spend their money poking around Heechee digs. There's a little of everything in it, from charts of the worked diggings and a large-scale Mercator map of Venus to samples of all the principal finds. I showed her the copy of the anisokinetic punch, and the original solid-state piezophone that had made its discoverer almost as permanently rich as the guys who marketed the punch. There were about a dozen fire-pearls, quarter-inch jobbies; they sat behind armor glass, on cushions, blazing away with their cold milky light. "They were what made the piezophone possible," I told her. "The machine itself, that's a human invention; but the fire-pearls are what makes it work—they convert pressure into electricity and vice versa."

"They're pretty," she said. "But why do they have to be protected like that? I saw bigger ones lying on a counter in the Spindle without anybody even watching them."

"That's a little different, Dorotha," I told her. "These are real."

She laughed out loud. I liked her laugh. No woman looks beautiful when she's laughing hard, and girls who worry about looking beautiful don't do it. Dorotha Keefer looked like a healthy, pretty

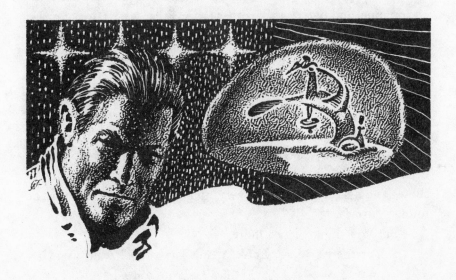

woman having a good time, which, when you come down to it, is about the best way for a woman to look.

She did not, however, look quite good enough to take my mind off my need for the money to buy a new liver, so I got down to business. "The little red marbles over there are blood-diamonds," I told her. "They're radioactive. Not so much that they'll hurt you, but they stay warm. Which is one way you can tell the real one from a fake: Anything over about three centimeters is a fake. A real one that big generates too much heat—the square-cube law, you know. So it melts."

"So the ones your friend was trying to sell me—"

"Were fakes. Right."

She nodded, still smiling. "What about what you were trying to sell us, Audee? Real or fake?"

The Third of Vastra's House had discreetly vanished by then, so I took a deep breath and told Dorotha the truth. Not the whole truth, maybe, but nothing but the truth.

"All this stuff here," I said, "is what thousands of people have found after a hell of a lot of digging. It's not much. The punch, the piezophone, and two or three other gadgets that we can make work; a few busted pieces of things that they're still studying; and some trinkets. That's it."

"That's the way I heard it," she said. "And one more thing. None of the discovery dates on these things is less than twenty years old." She was smarter and better informed than I had expected.

"And the conclusion you can draw from that," I agreed, "is that as nothing new has been found lately, the planet has probably been mined dry. You're right. That's what the evidence seems to show. The first diggers found everything useful that there was to be found . . . so far."

"But you think there's more."

"I *hope* there's more. Look. Item. The tunnel walls. You see they're all alike—the blue walls, perfectly smooth; the light coming from them that never varies; the hardness. How do you suppose the Heechee made them?"

"Why, I don't know."

"Neither do I. Or anybody else. But every Heechee tunnel is the same, and if you dig into them from the outside you find the same basic substrate rock, then a boundary layer that's sort of half wall-metal and half substrate, then the wall itself. Conclusion: The Heechee didn't dig the tunnels and then line them, they had something that crawled around underground like an earthworm, leaving these tunnels behind. And one other thing: they overdug. That's to say they dug lots of tunnels they didn't need, going nowhere, never used for anything. Does that suggest anything to you?"

"It must have been cheap and easy?" she guessed.

I nodded. "So it was probably an automatic machine, and there really ought to be at least one of them, somewhere on this planet, to find. Next item. The air. They breathed oxygen like we do, and they must have got it from somewhere. Where?"

"Why, there's oxygen in the atmosphere, isn't there?"

"Hardly any. Less than a half of a percent. And most of what there is isn't free oxygen; it's compounded into carbon dioxide and other garbage. There's no water vapor to speak of, either. Oh, a little—not as much as, for instance, sulfur dioxide. When water seeps out of the rock it doesn't come out as a fresh, clear spring. It goes into the air as vapor pretty fast. It rises—the water molecule being lighter than the carbon dioxide molecule. When it reaches a point where the sun can get at it it splits into hydrogen and oxygen. The oxygen and half the hydrogen mostly go into turning the sulfur dioxide into sulfuric acid. The rest of the hydrogen just escapes into space."

She was looking at me quizzically. "Audee," she said gently, "I already believe you're an expert on Venus."

I grinned. "But do you get the picture?"

"I think so. It looks pretty bad."

"It *is* pretty bad, but all the same the Heechee managed to get that little bit of oxygen out of the mixture, cheaply and easily—remember those extra tunnels they filled—along with inert gases like nitrogen—and they're present only in trace amounts—enough to make a breathing mixture. How? I don't know, but if there's a machine that did it I'd like to find that machine. Next item: aircraft. The Heechee flew around the surface of Venus a lot."

"So do you, Audee! Aren't you a pilot?"

"Airbody pilot, yes. But look what it takes to make an airbody go. There's a surface temperature of seven-thirty-five K, and not enough oxygen to keep a cigarette lit. So my airbody has to have two fuel tanks, one for the fuel, one for the thing to burn it with. That's not just oil and air, you know."

"It isn't?"

"Not here, Dorotha. Not at the kind of ambient temperatures we've got. It takes exotic fuels to get that hot. Did you ever hear of a fellow named Carnot?"

"Old-time scientist, was he? The Carnot cycle fellow?"

"Right again." That was the third time she'd surprised me, I noted cautiously. "The Carnot efficiency of an engine is expressed by its maximum temperature—the heat of combustion, let's say—divided by the temperature of its exhaust. Well, but the temperature of the exhaust can't be lower than the temperature of whatever it's exhausted into—otherwise you're not running an engine, you're running a refrigerator. And you've got that seven-thirty-five air temperature to fight, so even with special fuels you have basically a lousy engine. *Any* heat engine on Venus is lousy. Did you ever wonder why there are so few airbodies around? I don't mind; it helps to have something close to a monopoly. But the reason is that they're so damn expensive to run."

"And the Heechee did it better?"

"I *think* they did."

She laughed again, unexpectedly and once more very attractively. "Why, you poor fellow," she said in good humor, "you're hooked on the stuff you sell, aren't you? You think that one of these days you're going to find the mother tunnel and pick up a few billion dollars' worth of Heechee stuff!"

I wasn't pleased with the way she put that. I wasn't all that happy with the meeting I had set up with Vastra's Third, for that matter; I'd figured that, away from her boyfriend, I could pick this Dorotha Keefer's brains about him pretty easily. It wasn't working out that way. She was making me aware of her as a person, which was an undesirable development in itself—you can't treat a mark as a mark if you think of him, or her, as a fellow human being.

Worse than that, she was making me take a good look at myself.

So I just said, "You may be right. But I'm sure going to give it a good try."

"You're angry, aren't you?"

"No," I lied, "but maybe a little tired. And we've got a long trip tomorrow, so I'd better take you back to the Spindle, Miss Keefer."

My airbody was roped down at the edge of the spacepad and was reached the same way the spacepad was reached: elevator to the

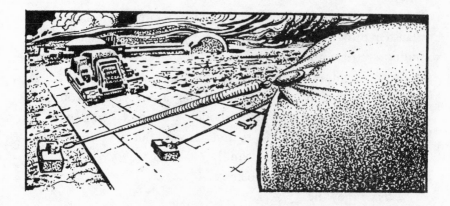

surface lock, then a sealed tractor cab to carry us across the dry, rocky, tortured surface of Venus, peeling away under the high-density wind. Normally I kept the airbody under a lashed-down foam housing, of course. You don't leave anything free and exposed on the surface of Venus if you want to find it intact when you get back to it, not even if it's made of chrome steel. I'd had the foam stripped off first thing that morning, when I checked it out and loaded supplies. Now it was ready. I could see it from the bull's-eye ports of the crawler, through the howling, green-yellow murk outside.

Cochenour and the girl could have seen it too, if they'd known where to look, but they might not have recognized it as something that would fly.

"Did you and Dorrie have a fight?" Cochenour screamed in my ear.

"No fight," I screamed back.

"Don't care if you did. Just wanted to know. You don't have to like each other, just so you do what I want you to do." He was silent for a moment, resting his vocal cords. "Jesus. What a wind."

"Zephyr," I told him. I didn't say any more; he would find out for himself. The area around the spacepad is a sort of natural calm area, by Venusian standards. Orographic lift throws the meanest of the winds up over the pad, and all we get is a sort of confused back eddy. That makes taking off and landing relatively easy. The bad part of that is that some of the heavy metal compounds in the air settle out on the pad. What passes for air on Venus has layers of red mercuric sulfide and mercurous chloride in the lower reaches, and when you get above them to those pretty fluffy clouds tourists see on the way down, you find that some of them are droplets of sulfuric and hydrochloric and hydrofluoric acid.

But there are tricks to that, too. Navigation over Venus takes 3-D skills. It's easy enough to proceed from Point A to Point B on the surface. Your transponders will link you to the radio range and map your position continuously on the charts. What's hard is to find the right altitude. That takes experience and maybe intuition, and that's why my airbody and I were worth a million dollars to people like Boyce Cochenour.

By then we were at the airbody, and the telescoping snout from the crawler was poking out to its lock. Cochenour was staring out the bull's-eye. "It doesn't have any wings!" he shouted, as though I was cheating him.

"It doesn't have sails or snow chains either," I shouted back. "Get aboard if you want to talk! It'll be easier in the airbody."

We climbed through the little snout, I unlocked the entrance, and we got aboard without much trouble.

We didn't even have the kind of trouble that I might have made for myself. You see, an airbody is a big thing on Venus. I was damn lucky to have been able to acquire it, and, well, I won't beat around the bush, you could say I loved it. Mine could have held ten people, without equipment. With what Sub Vastra's outfitting shop had sold us and Local 88 had certified as essential to have on board, it was crowded with just the three of us.

I was prepared for at least sarcasm. But Cochenour merely looked around long enough to find the best bunk, strode over to it, and claimed it as his. The girl was acting like a good sport about all the inconveniences. And there I was, left with my glands charged up for hostile criticism, and nobody criticizing.

It was a lot quieter inside the airbody. You could hear the noise of the winds right enough, but it was only annoying. I passed out high-filter earplugs, and with them in place the noise was hardly even annoying.

"Sit down and strap in," I ordered, and when they were stowed away I took off.

At ninety thousand millibars, wings aren't just useless, they're poison. My airbody had all the lift it needed, built right into its seashell-shaped hull. I fed the double fuel mixture into the thermo-jets, we bounced across the reasonably flat ground at the edge of the spacepad (it was bulldozed once a week, which is how it stayed reasonably flat), and we were zooming off into the wild yellow-green yonder—a moment later, into the wild brown-gray yonder—after a run of no more than fifty meters.

Cochenour had fastened his harness loosely to be comfortable. I enjoyed hearing him yell as he was thrown about in the savage, short-period turbulence. It wouldn't kill him, and it only lasted for a few moments. At a thousand meters I found our part of Venus's semipermanent atmospheric inversion, and the turbulence dropped to where I could take off my belt and stand.

I took the plugs out of my ears and motioned to Cochenour and the girl to do the same.

He was rubbing his head where he'd bounced into an overhead chart rack, but he was grinning a little. "Pretty exciting," he admitted, fumbling in his pocket. "All right if I smoke?"

"They're your lungs."

He grinned more widely. "They are now," he agreed. "Say, why didn't you give us those earplugs while we were in the tractor?"

There is, as you might say, a tide in the affairs of guides, where you either let them flood you with questions and then spend the whole time explaining what that funny little dial means when it turns red . . . or you keep your mouth shut and go on to do your work and make your fortune. What it came down to was a choice: Was I going to come out of this liking Cochenour and his girlfriend, or not?

If I was, I should try to be civil to them. More than civil. Living, the three of us, for three weeks in a space about as big as an apartment kitchenette meant that everybody would have to work real hard at being nice to everybody else, if we were going to come back without total hatred. And as I was the one who was being paid to be nice, I should be the one to set an example.

On the other hand, the Cochenours of the world are sometimes just not likable. If that was going to be the case, the less talk the better, and I should slide questions like that off with something like, "I forgot."

But he hadn't actually gone out of his way to be unpleasant. The girl had even actually attempted friendliness. So I opted for courtesy. "Well, that's an interesting thing. You see, you hear by differences in pressure. While the airbody was taking off, the plugs filtered out part of the sound—the pressure waves—but when I yelled at you to belt up, the plugs passed the overpressure of my voice and you could hear easily enough. However, there's a limit. Past about a hundred and twenty decibels—that's a unit of sound—"

"I know what a decibel is," Cochenour growled.

"Right. Past a hundred and twenty or so the eardrum just doesn't respond anymore. So in the crawler it was just too loud. You not only got sound in through the hull, it came up from the ground, conducted by the treads. If you'd had the plugs in you wouldn't even have been able to hear—well, anything at all," I finished lamely.

Dorotha had been listening while she repaired her eye makeup. "Anything like what?" she demanded.

I decided to think of them as friends, at least for the time being. "Like orders to get into your heatsuits. In case of accident, I mean. A gust could've tipped that crawler right over, or sometimes solid objects come flying over the hills and hit you before you know it."

She was shaking her head, but she was laughing. "Lovely place you took us to, Boyce," she commented.

He wasn't paying any attention. He had something else on his mind. "Why aren't you flying this thing?" he demanded.

I got up and activated the virtual globe. "Right," I said. "It's time we talked about that. Just now my airbody's on autopilot, heading in the general direction of this quadrant down here. We have to decide on a specific destination."

Dorrie Keefer was inspecting the globe. It isn't real, of course; it's just a three-dimensional image that hangs in the air, and you can poke your finger right through it. "Venus doesn't really look like much," she commented.

"Those lines you see," I explained, "are just radio-range markers; you won't see them looking out the window. Venus doesn't

have any oceans, and it isn't cut up into countries, so making a map of it isn't quite what you'd expect on Earth. See this bright spot here? That's us. Now look."

I overlaid the radio-range grid and the contour colors with geological data. "Those blobby circles are mascon markers. You know what a mascon is?"

"A concentration of mass. A lump of heavy stuff," she offered.

"Fine. Now see what happens when I phase in the locations of known Heechee digs."

When I hit the control the digs appeared as golden patterns, like worms crawling across the planet. Dorotha said at once, "They're all in the mascons."

Cochenour gave her a look of approval, and so did I. "Not quite all," I corrected. "But damn near. Why? I don't know. Nobody knows. The mascons are mostly older, denser rock—basalt and so on—and maybe the Heechee felt safer with strong, dense rock around them." In my correspondence with Professor Hegramet back on Earth, in the days when I didn't have a dying liver in my gut and thus could afford to take an interest in abstract knowledge, we had kicked around the possibility that the Heechee digging machines would only work in dense rock, or rock of a certain chemical composition. But I wasn't prepared to discuss some of the ideas I'd gotten from Professor Hegramet with them.

I rotated the virtual globe slightly by turning a dial. "See over here, where we are now. This formation's Alpha Regio. There's the big digging which we just came out of. You can see the shape of the Spindle. That particular mascon where the Spindle is is called Serendip; it was discovered by a hesperological—"

"Hesperological?"

"By a geological team studying Venus, which makes it a hesperological team. They detected the mass concentration from orbit, then after the landings they drilled out a core sample there and hit the first Heechee dig. Now these other digs you see in the northern high latitudes are all in this one bunch of associated mascons. There

43

are interventions of less dense rock between them, and they tunnel right through to connect, but they're almost all right in the mascons."

"They're all north," Cochenour said sharply. "We're going south. Why?"

It was interesting that he could read the virtual globe, but I didn't say so. I only said, "The ones that are marked are no good. They've been probed already."

"Some of them look even bigger than the Spindle."

"A hell of a lot bigger, right. But there's nothing much in them, or anyway not much chance that anything in them is in good enough shape to bother with. Subsurface fluids filled them up a hundred thousand years ago, maybe more. A lot of good men have gone broke trying to pump one out and excavate, without finding anything. Ask me. I was one of them."

"I didn't know Venus had any liquid water," Cochenour objected.

"I didn't say water, did I? But as a matter of fact some of it was, or anyway a sort of oozy mud. Apparently water cooks out of the rocks and has a transit time, getting to the surface, of some thousands of years before it seeps out, boils off, and cracks to hydrogen and oxygen and gets lost. In case you didn't know it, there's some under the Spindle. It's what you were drinking, and what you were breathing, while you were there."

"We weren't breathing water," he corrected.

"No, of course not. We were breathing air that we made. But sometimes the tunnels still have kept their air—I mean the original stuff, the air the Heechee left behind them. Of course, after a few hundred thousand years they generally turn into ovens. Then they tend to bake everything organic away. Maybe that's why we've found so little of, let's say, animal remains—they've been cremated. So—sometimes you might find air in a dig, but I've never heard of anybody finding drinkable water in one."

Dorotha said, "Boyce, this is all very interesting, but I'm hot and dirty and all this talk about water's getting to me. Can I change the subject for a minute?"

Cochenour barked; it wasn't really a laugh. "Subliminal prompting, Walthers, don't you agree? And a little old-fashioned prudery too, I expect. I think what Dorrie really wants to do is go to the toilet."

Given a little encouragement from the girl, I would have been mildly embarrassed for her. She was evidently used to Cochenour. She only said, "If we're going to live in this thing for three weeks, I'd like to know what it offers."

"Certainly, Miss Keefer," I said.

"Dorotha. Dorrie, if you like it better."

"Sure, Dorrie. Well, you see what you've got. There are five bunks; they partition to sleep ten if wanted, but we don't want. Two shower stalls. They don't look big enough to soap yourself in, but they'll do the job if you work at it. Two chemical toilets in those cubbies. Kitchen over there—stove and storage, anyway. Pick the bunk you like, Dorrie. There's a screen arrangement that comes down when you want it for changing clothes and so on, or just if you don't want to look at the rest of us for a while."

Cochenour said, "Go on, Dorrie, do what you want to do. I want Walthers to show me how to fly this thing anyway."

It wasn't a bad start to the trip. I've had worse. I've had some real traumatic times, parties that came aboard drunk and steadily got drunker, couples that fought each other every waking moment and only got together long enough so they could fight in a united front against me. This trip didn't look bad at all, even apart from the fact that I hoped it was going to save my life for me.

You don't need much skill to fly an airbody—at least, just to make it move in the direction you want to go. In Venus's atmosphere there is lift to spare. You don't worry about things like stalling out; and anyway the automatic controls do most of your thinking for you.

Cochenour learned fast. It turned out he had flown everything that moved through the air on Earth, and operated one-man submersibles, as well, in the deep-sea oil fields of his youth. He understood as soon as I mentioned it to him that the hard part of pilotage on Venus was selecting the right flying level, and anticipating when you'd have to change it. But he also understood that he wasn't going to learn that in one day. Or even in three weeks. "What the hell, Walthers," he said cheerfully enough. "At least I can make it go where I have to—in case you get trapped in a tunnel. Or shot by a jealous husband."

I gave him the smile that little pleasantry was worth, which wasn't much. "The other thing I can do," he went on, "is cook. Unless you're really good at it? No, I thought not. Well, I paid too much for this stomach to fill it with hash, so I'll make the meals. That's a little skill Dorrie never got around to learning. It was the same with her grandmother. The most beautiful woman in the world, but she had the idea that was all she had to be to own it."

I put that aside to sort out later. He was full of little unexpected

46

things, this ninety-year-old young athlete. He said, "All right. Now, while Dorrie's using up all the water in the shower—"

"Not to worry; it recycles."

"Anyway. While she's cleaning up, finish your little lecture on where we're going."

"Right." I spun the globe a little. The bright spot that was us had been heading steadily south while we were talking. "See that cluster where our track intersects those grid marks, just short of Lise Meitner?"

"Who's Lise Meitner?" he grunted.

"Somebody they named that formation after, that's all I know. Do you see where I'm pointing?"

"Yeah. Those five big mascons close together. No diggings indicated. Is that where we're going?"

"In a general way, yes."

"Why in a general way?"

"Well," I said, "there's one little thing I didn't tell you. I'm assuming you won't jump salty over it, because then I'll have to get salty, too, and tell you you should have taken the trouble to learn more about Venus before you decided to explore it."

He studied me appraisingly for a moment. Dorrie came quietly out of the shower in a long robe, her hair in a towel, and stood near him, watching me. "That depends a lot on what you didn't tell me, friend," he said—not sounding friendly.

"That part there is the South Polar Security Area," I said. "That's where the Defense boys keep the missile range and the biggest part of their weapons development areas. And civilians aren't allowed to enter."

He was glowering at the map. "But there's only that one little piece of a mascon that isn't off limits!"

"And that little piece," I said, "is where we're going."

VI

For a man more than ninety years old, Boyce Cochenour was spry. I don't mean just that he was healthy. Full Medical will do that for you, because you just replace whatever wears out or begins to look tacky. You can't replace the brain, though. So what you usually see in the very rich old ones is a bronzed, muscular body that shakes and hesitates and drops things.

About that Cochenour had been very lucky.

He was going to be abrasive company for three weeks. He'd already insisted I show him how to pilot an airbody, and he had learned fast. When I decided to use a little flight time to give the cooling system a somewhat premature thousand-hour check, he helped me pull the covers, check the refrigerant levels, and clean the filters. Then he decided to cook us lunch.

Dorrie Keefer took over as my helper while I moved some of the supplies around, getting the autosonic probes out. At the steady noise level of the inside of an airbody, our normal voices wouldn't carry to Cochenour, a couple of meters away at the stove. I thought of pumping the girl about him while we checked the probes. I decided against it. I already knew the important thing about Cochenour, namely that with any luck he might be going to pay for my new liver. I didn't need to know what he and Dorrie thought about when they thought about each other.

So what we talked about was the probes. About how they would fire percussive charges into the Venusian rock and time the returning echoes. And about what the chances were of finding something really good. ("Well, what are the chances of winning a sweepstakes? For any individual ticket holder they're bad. But there's always one winner somewhere!") And about what had made me come to Venus in the first place. I mentioned my father's name, but she'd never heard of the deputy governor of Texas. Too young, no doubt. Anyway she had been born and bred in southern Ohio, where Cochenour had worked as a kid and to which he'd returned as a

billionaire. She told me, without my urging, how he'd been building a new processing center there, and how many headaches that had been—trouble with the unions, trouble with the banks, bad trouble with the government—and so he'd decided to take a good long time off to loaf. I looked over to where he was stirring up a sauce and said, "He loafs harder than anybody else I ever saw."

"He's a work addict, Audee. I imagine that's how he got rich in the first place." The airbody lurched, and I dropped everything to jump for the controls. I heard Cochenour howl behind me, but I was busy locating a better transit level. By the time I had climbed a thousand meters and reset the autopilot he was rubbing his wrist and swearing at me.

"Sorry," I said.

He said dourly, "I don't mind your scalding the skin off my arm. I can always buy more skin, but you nearly made me spill the gravy."

I checked the virtual globe. The bright ship marker was two-thirds of the way to our destination. "Is lunch about ready?" I asked. "We'll be there in an hour."

For the first time he looked startled. "So soon? I thought you said this thing was subsonic."

"I did. You're on Venus, Mr. Cochenour. At this level the speed of sound is a lot faster than on Earth."

He looked thoughtful, but all he said was "Well, we can eat any minute." Later he said, while we were finishing up, "I think maybe I don't know as much about this planet as I might. If you want to give us the guide's lecture, we'll listen."

"You already know the outlines," I told him. "Say, you're a great cook, Mr. Cochenour. I know I packed all the provisions, but I don't even know what this is I'm eating."

"If you come to my office in Cincinnati," he said, "you can ask for Mr. Cochenour, but while we're living in each other's armpits you might as well call me Boyce. And if you like the fricassee, why aren't you eating it?"

The answer was, because it might kill me. I didn't want to get

50

into a discussion that might lead to why I needed his fee so badly. "Doctor's orders," I said, "Have to lay off the fats for a while. I think he thinks I'm putting on too much weight."

Cochenour looked at me appraisingly, but all he said was "The lecture?"

"Well, let's start with the most important part," I said, carefully pouring coffee. "While we're inside this airbody you can do what you like—walk around, eat, drink, smoke if you got 'em, whatever. The cooling system is built for more than three times this many people, plus their cooking and appliance loads, with a safety factor of two. Air and water, more than we'd need for two months. Fuel, enough for three round trips plus maneuvering. If anything went wrong we'd yell for help and somebody would come and get us in a couple of hours at the most. Probably it would be the Defense boys, because they're closest and they have really *fast* airbodies. The worst thing would be if the hull breached and the whole Venusian atmosphere tried to come in. If that happened fast we'd just be dead. It never happens fast, though. We'd have time to get into the suits, and we can live in them for thirty hours. Long before that we'd be picked up."

"Assuming, of course, that nothing went wrong with the radio at the same time."

"Right. Assuming that. You know that you can get killed anywhere, if enough accidents happen at once."

He poured himself another cup of coffee and tipped a little brandy into it. "Go on."

"Well, outside the airbody it's a lot trickier. You've only got the suit to keep you alive, and its useful life, as I say, is only thirty hours. It's a question of refrigeration. You can carry plenty of air and water, and you don't have to worry about food on that time scale, but it takes a lot of compact energy to get rid of the diffuse energy all around you. That means fuel. The cooling systems use up a lot of fuel, and when that's gone you'd better be back in the airbody. Heat isn't the worst way to die. You pass out before you begin to hurt. But in the end you're dead.

"The other thing is, you want to check your suit every time you put it on. Pressure it up, and watch the gauge for leaks. I'll check, too, but *don't rely on me*. It's your life. And watch the face-plates. They're pretty strong—you can drive nails with them without breaking them—but if they're hit hard enough by something that's also hard enough they can crack all the same. That way you're dead, too."

Dorrie asked quietly, "Have you ever lost a tourist?"

"No." But then I added, "Others have. Five or six get killed every year."

"I'll play at those odds," Cochenour said seriously. "Anyway, that wasn't the lecture I wanted, Audee. I mean, I certainly want to hear how to stay alive, but I assume you would have told us all this before we left the ship anyway. What I really wanted to know was how come you picked this particular mascon to prospect."

This old geezer with the muscle-beach body was beginning to bother me, with his disturbing habit of asking the questions I didn't want to answer. There definitely was a reason why I had picked this site. It had to do with about five years of study, a lot of digging, and about a quarter of a million dollars' worth of correspondence, at space-mail rates, with people like Professor Hegramet back on Earth.

But I didn't want to tell him all my reasons. There were about a dozen sites that I really wanted to explore. If this happened to be one of the payoff places, he would come out of it a lot richer than I would—that's what the contracts you sign say: forty percent to the charterer, five percent to the guide, the rest to the government—and that should be enough for him. If this one happened not to pay off, I didn't want him taking some other guide to one of the others I'd marked.

So I only said, "Call it an informed guess. I promised you a good shot at a tunnel that's never been opened, and I hope to keep my promise. And now let's get the food put away; we're within ten minutes of where we're going."

With everything strapped down and ourselves belted up, we dropped out of the relatively calm layers into the big surface winds again.

We were over the big south-central massif, about the same elevation as the lands surrounding the Spindle. That's the elevation where most of the action is on Venus. Down in the lowlands and the deep rift valleys the pressures run a hundred and twenty thousand millibars and up. My airbody wouldn't take any of that for very long. Neither would anybody else's, except for a few of the special research and military types. Fortunately, it seemed the Heechee didn't care for the lowlands, either. Nothing of theirs has ever been located much below ninety-bar. Doesn't mean it isn't there, of course.

Anyway, I verified our position on the virtual globe and on the detail charts, and deployed the first three autosonic probes.

The winds threw them all over the place as soon as they dropped free. That was all right. It doesn't much matter where the probes land, within broad limits, which is a good thing. They dropped like javelins at first, then flew around like straws in the wind until their little rockets cut in and the ground-seeking controls fired them to the surface.

Every one embedded itself properly. You aren't always that lucky, so it was a good start.

I verified their position on the detail charts. It was close enough to an equilateral triangle, which is about how you want them. Then I made sure everybody was really strapped in, opened the scanning range, and began circling around.

"Now what?" bellowed Cochenour. I noticed the girl had put her earplugs back in, but he wasn't willing to risk missing a thing.

"Now we wait for the probes to feel around for Heechee tunnels. It'll take a couple of hours." While I was talking I brought the airbody down through the surface layers. Now we were being thrown around by the gusts. The buffeting got pretty bad.

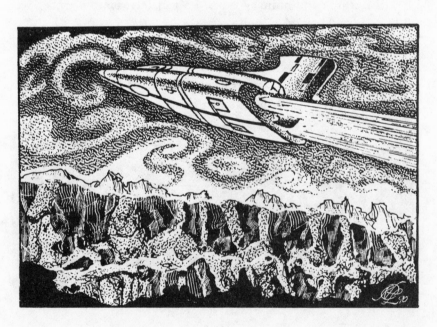

But I found what I was looking for, a surface formation like a blind arroyo, and tucked us into it with only one or two bad moments. Cochenour was watching very carefully, and I grinned to myself. This was where pilotage counted, not en route or at the prepared pads over the Spindle. When he could do what I was doing now he could get along without someone like me—not before.

Our position looked all right, so I fired four hold-downs, tethered stakes with explosive heads that opened out in the ground. I winched them tight, and all of them held.

That was also a good sign. Reasonably pleased with myself, I released the belt catches and stood up. "We're here for at least a day or two," I told them. "More if we're lucky. How did you like the ride?"

Dorrie was taking the earplugs out, now that the protecting walls of the arroyo had cut the thundering down to a mere scream. "I'm glad I don't get airsick," she said.

Cochenour was thinking, not talking. He was studying the air-body controls while he lit another cigarette.

Dorotha said, "One question, Audee. Why couldn't we stay up where it's quieter?"

"Fuel. I carry enough to get us around, but not to hover for days. Is the noise bothering you?"

She made a face.

"You'll get used to it. It's like living next to a spaceport. At first you wonder how anybody stands the noise for a single hour. After you've been there a week you'll miss it if it stops."

She moved over to the bull's-eye and gazed pensively out at the landscape. We'd crossed over into the night portion, and there wasn't much to see but dust and small objects whirling around through our external light beams. "It's that first week I'm worrying about," she said.

I flicked on the probe readout. The little percussive heads were firing their slap-charges and measuring each other's echoes, but it was too early to see anything. The screen was barely beginning to build up a shadowy pattern. There were more holes than detail.

Cochenour finally spoke up. "How long until you can make some sense out of the readout?" he demanded. Another point: he hadn't asked what it was.

"Depends on how close and how big anything is. You can make a guess in an hour or so, but I like all the data I can get. Six or eight hours, I'd say. There's no hurry."

He growled, "*I'm* in a hurry, Walthers."

The girl cut in. "What should we do, Audee? Play three-handed bridge?"

"Whatever you want, but I'd advise some sleep. I've got pills if you want them. If we do find anything—and remember, the odds are really rotten on the first try—we'll want to be wide awake for a while."

"All right," Dorotha said, reaching out for the spansules, but Cochenour stopped her.

"What about you?" he demanded.

"I'll sack in pretty soon. I'm waiting for something."

He didn't ask what. Probably, I thought, because he already knew. I decided that when I did hit my bunk I wouldn't take a sleepy pill right away. This Cochenour was not only the richest tourist I had ever guided, he was one of the best informed. And I wanted to think about that for a while.

So none of us went right to sleep, and what I was waiting for took almost an hour to come. The boys at the base were getting a little sloppy; they should have been after us before this.

The radio buzzed and then blared. "Unidentified vessel at one three five, zero seven, four eight, and seven two, five one, five four! Please identify yourself and state your purpose."

Cochenour looked up inquiringly from his gin game with the girl. I smiled reassuringly. "As long as they're saying 'please' there's no problem," I told him, and opened the transmitter.

"This is pilot Audee Walthers, airbody Poppa Tare Nine One,

out of the Spindle. We are licensed and have filed approved flight plans. I have two Terry tourists aboard, purpose recreational exploration."

"Acknowledged. Please wait," blared the radio. The military always broadcasts at maximum gain. Hangover from drill-sergeant days, no doubt.

I turned off the microphone and told my passengers, "They're checking our flight plan. Nothing to worry about."

In a moment the Defense communicator came back, loud as ever. "You are eleven point four kilometers bearing two eight three degrees from terminator of a restricted area. Proceed with caution. Under Military Regulations One Seven and One Eight, Sections—"

"I know the drill," I cut in. "I have my guide's license and have explained the restrictions to the passengers."

"Acknowledged," blared the radio. "We will keep you under surveillance. If you observe vessels or parties on the surface, they are our perimeter teams. Do not interfere with them in any way. Respond at once to any request for identification or information." The carrier buzz cut off.

"They act nervous," Cochenour said.

"No. That's how they always are. They're used to seeing people like us around. They've got nothing else to do with their time, that's all."

Dorrie said hesitantly, "Audee, you told them you'd explained the restrictions to us. I don't remember that part."

"Oh, I explained them, all right. We stay out of the restricted area, because if we don't they'll start shooting. That is the Whole of the Law."

VII

I set a wake-up for four hours, and the others heard me moving around and got up, too. Dorrie fetched us coffee from the warmer, and we stood drinking it and looking at the patterns the probe computer had traced.

I took several minutes to study them, although the patterns were clear enough at first look. They showed eight major anomalies that could have been Heechee warrens. One was almost right outside our door. We wouldn't have to move the airbody to dig for it.

I showed them the anomalies, one by one. Cochenour just studied them thoughtfully. Dorotha asked, "You mean all of those blobs are unexplored tunnels?"

"No. Wish they were. But even if they were: One, any or all of them could have been explored by somebody who didn't go to the trouble of recording it. Two, they don't have to be tunnels. They could be fracture faults, or dikes, or little rivers of some kind of molten material that ran out of somewhere and hardened and got covered over a billion years ago. The only thing we know for sure so far is that there probably aren't any unexplored tunnels in this area *except* in those eight places."

"So what do we do?"

"We dig. And then we see what we've got."

Cochenour asked, "Where do we dig?"

I pointed right next to the bright delta shape of our airbody. "Right here."

"Is that the best bet?"

"Well, not necessarily." I considered what to tell him and decided to experiment with the truth. "There are three traces altogether that look like better bets than the others—here, I'll mark them." I keyed the chart controls, and the three good traces immediately displayed letters: A, B, and C. "A is the one that runs right under the arroyo here, so we'll dig it first."

"The brightest ones are best, is that it?"

I nodded.

"But C over here is the brightest of the lot. Why don't we dig that first?"

I chose my words carefully. "Partly because we'd have to move the airbody. Partly because it's on the outside perimeter of the survey area; that means the results aren't as reliable as right around the ship. But those aren't the most important reasons. The most important reason is that C is on the edge of the line our itchy-fingered Defense friends are telling us to stay away from."

Cochenour snickered incredulously. "Are you telling me that if you find a real untouched Heechee tunnel you'll stay out of it just because some soldier tells you it's a no-no?"

I said, "The problem doesn't arise. We have seven legal anomalies to look at. Also—the military will be checking us from time to time. Particularly in the next day or two."

"All right," Cochenour insisted, "suppose we come up empty on the legal ones. What then?"

"I never borrow trouble."

"But suppose."

"Damn it, Boyce! How do I know?"

He gave it up then, but winked at Dorrie and chuckled. "What did I tell you, honey? He's a bigger bandit than I am!"

But she was looking at me, and what she said was "Why are you that color?"

I fobbed her off, but when I looked in the mirror I could see that even the whites of my eyes were turning yellowish.

The next few hours we were too busy to talk about theoretical possibilities. We had some concrete facts to worry about.

The biggest concrete fact was an awful lot of high-temperature, high-pressure gas that we had to keep from killing us. That was what the heatsuits were for. My own suit was custom-made, of course, and needed only the fittings and tanks to be checked. Boyce and the girl had rental units. I'd paid top dollar for them, and they were good. But good isn't perfect. I had them in and out of the suits half a dozen times, checking the fit and making adjustments until they were as right as I could get them. The suits were laminated twelve-ply, with nine degrees of freedom at the essential joints, and

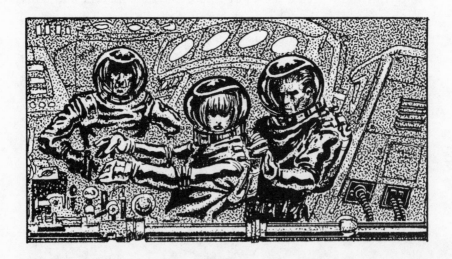

their own little fuel batteries. They wouldn't fail. I wasn't worried about failure. What I was worried about was comfort, because a very small itch or rub can get serious when there's no way to stop it.

Finally they were good enough for a trial. We all huddled in the lock and opened the port to the surface of Venus.

We were still in darkness, but there's so much scatter from the sun that it doesn't get really dark ever. I let them practice walking around the airbody, leaning into the wind, bracing themselves against the hold-downs and the side of the ship, while I got ready to dig.

I hauled out our first instant igloo, dragged it into position, and ignited it. As it smoldered it puffed up like the children's toy that

used to be called a Pharaoh's Serpent, producing a light yet tough ash that grew up around the digging site and joined in a seamless dome at the top. I had already emplaced the digging torch and the crawl-through lock. As the ash grew I manhandled the lock to get a close union and managed to get a perfect join the first time.

Dorrie and Cochenour stayed out of the way, watching from the ship through their plug windows. Then I keyed the radio on. "You want to come in and watch me start it up?" I shouted.

Inside the helmets, they both nodded their heads; I could just see the bobbing motion through the plugs. "Come on, then," I yelled, and wiggled through the crawl lock. I signed for them to leave it open as they followed me in.

With the three of us and the digging equipment in it, the igloo was even more crowded than the airbody had been. They backed away as far from me as they could get, bent against the arc of the igloo wall, while I started up the augers, checked that they were vertical, and watched the first castings begin to spiral out of the cut.

The foam igloo reflects a lot of sound and absorbs even more. All the same, the din inside the igloo was a lot worse than in the howling winds outside; cutters are *noisy*. When I thought they'd seen enough to satisfy them for the moment, I waved them out of the crawl-through, followed, sealed it behind us, and led them back into the airbody.

"So far, so good," I said, twisting off the helmet and loosening the suit. "We've got about forty meters to cut, I think. Might as well wait in here as out there."

"How long will it take?"

"Maybe an hour. You can do what you like; what I'm going to do is take a shower. Then we'll see how far we've got."

That was one of the nice things about having only three people aboard: we didn't have to worry much about water discipline. It's astonishing how a quick wet-down revives you after coming out of a heatsuit. When I'd finished mine I felt ready for anything.

I was even prepared to eat some of Boyce Cochenour's three-thousand-calorie gourmet cooking, but fortunately it wasn't necessary. Dorrie had taken over the kitchen, and what she laid out was simple, light, and reasonably nontoxic. On cooking like hers I might be able to survive long enough to collect my charter fee. It crossed my mind to wonder why she was a health nut, but then I thought,

of course, she wants to keep Cochenour alive. With all his spare parts, no doubt he had dietary problems worse than mine.

Well, not "worse," exactly. At least he probably wasn't quite as likely to die of them.

The Venusian surface at that point was little more than ashy sand. The augers chewed it out very rapidly. Too rapidly, in fact. When I went back into the igloo it was filled almost solid with castings. I had a devil of a job getting to the machines so that I could rotate the auger to pump the castings out through the crawl lock.

It was a dirty job, but it didn't take long.

I didn't bother to go back into the airbody. I reported over the radio to Boyce and the girl, whom I could see staring out of the bull's-eyes at me. I told them I thought we were getting close.

But I didn't tell them exactly how close.

Actually, we were only a meter or so from the indicated depth of the anomaly, so close that I didn't bother to auger all the castings out. I just made enough room to maneuver around inside the igloo.

Then I redirected the augers. And in five minutes the castings were beginning to come up with the pale blue Heechee-metal glimmer that was the sign of a real tunnel.

VIII

About ten minutes later, I keyed my helmet transmitter on and shouted, "Boyce! Dorrie! We've hit a tunnel!"

Either they were already in their suits or they dressed faster than any maze-rat. I unsealed the crawl-through and wriggled out to help them . . . and they were already coming out of the airbody, pulling themselves hand over hand against the wind toward me.

They were both yelling questions and congratulations, but I

stopped them. "Inside," I ordered. "You can see for yourself." As a matter of fact, they didn't have to go that far. They could see the blue color as soon as they knelt to enter the crawl-through.

I followed and sealed the outer port of the crawl-through behind me. The reason for that is simple enough. As long as the tunnel isn't breached, it doesn't matter what you do. But the interior of a Heechee tunnel that has remained inviolate is at a pressure only slightly above Earth-normal. Without the sealed dome of the igloo, the minute you crack the casing you let the whole ninety-thousand-millibar atmosphere of Venus pour in, heat and ablation and corrosive chemicals and all. If the tunnel is empty, or if what's in it is simple, sturdy stuff, there might not be any harm. But there are a couple of dozen mysterious chunks of scrap in the museums that might have been interesting machines—if whoever found them hadn't let the atmosphere in to squeeze them into junk. If you hit the jackpot, you can destroy in a second what has waited hundreds of thousands of years to be discovered.

We gathered around the shaft, and I pointed down. The augers had left a clean shaft, about seventy centimeters by a little over a hundred, with rounded edges. At the bottom you could see the cold blue glow of the outside of the tunnel, only pocked by the augers and blotched by the loose castings I hadn't bothered to get out.

"Now what?" Cochenour demanded. His voice was hoarse with excitement—natural enough, I guessed.

"Now we burn our way in."

I backed my clients as far away as they could get inside the igloo, pressed against the remaining heap of castings. Then I unlimbered the fire-jets. I'd already hung shear-legs over the shaft. The jets slipped right down on their cable until they were just a few centimeters above the round of the tunnel.

Then I fired them up.

You wouldn't think that anything a human being might do would make anything hotter than Venus does already, but the fire-jets were something special. In the small space of the igloo the heat

flamed up and around us. Our heatsuit cooling systems were overwhelmed in a moment.

Dorrie gasped, "Oh! I—I think I'm going to—"

Cochenour grabbed her arm. "Faint if you want to," he said fiercely, "but don't get sick inside your suit. Walthers! How long does this go on?"

It was as hard for me as it was for them. Practice doesn't get you used to something like standing in front of a blast furnace with the doors off the hinges. "Maybe a minute," I gasped. "Hold on—it's all right."

It actually took a little more than that, maybe ninety seconds. My suit telltales were shouting overload alarm for more than half of that time. But the suits were built for these temporary overloads. As long as we didn't cook inside them, the suits themselves would survive.

Then we were through. A half-meter circular section of the tunnel roof sagged, fell at one side, and hung there, swaying.

I turned off the jets. We all breathed hard for a couple of minutes, while the suit coolers gradually caught up with the load.

"Wow," said Dorotha. "That was pretty rough."

In the light that splashed up out of the shaft I could see that
Cochenour was frowning. I didn't say anything. I just gave the jets
another five-second burn to cut away the rest of the circular section.
It fell free to the tunnel floor, with a smack like rock.

Then I turned on my helmet radio.

"There's no pressure differential," I said.

Cochenour's frown didn't change, nor did he speak.

"That means this one has been breached," I went on. "Somebody found it, opened it up—probably cleaned it out, if there ever
was anything here—and just didn't report it. Let's go back to the
airbody and get cleaned up."

Dorotha shrieked, "Audee, what's the matter with you? I want
to go down there and see what's inside!"

"Shut up, Dorrie," Cochenour said bitterly. "Don't you hear
what he's saying? This one's a washout."

Well, there's always the chance that a breached tunnel might
have been opened by some seismological event, not a maze-rat with
a cutting torch. If so, there might possibly be something in it worth
having anyway. And I didn't have the heart to kill all Dorotha's
enthusiasm with one blow.

So we did swing down the cable, one by one, into the Heechee dig. We looked around. It was wholly bare, as most of them are, as far as we could see. That wasn't actually very far. The other thing wrong with a breached tunnel is that you need special equipment to explore it. With the overloads they'd already had, our suits were all right for another few hours but not much more than that.

So we tramped down the tunnel about a kilometer and found bare walls, chopped-off struts on the glowing blue walls that might once have held something—and nothing movable. Not even junk.

Then they were both willing to tramp back and climb up the cable to the airbody. Cochenour made it on his own. So did Dorrie, though I was standing by to help her; she did it all hand over hand, using the stirrups spaced along the cable.

We cleaned up and made ourselves a meal. We had to eat, but Cochenour was not in a mood for his gourmet exhibition. Silently, Dorotha threw tablets into the cooker and we fed gloomily on pre-fabs.

"Well, that's only the first one," she said at last, determined to be sunny about it. "And it's only our second day."

Cochenour said, "Shut up, Dorrie. If there's one thing I'm not, it's a good loser." He was staring at the probe trace, still displayed on the screen. "Walthers, how many tunnels are unmarked but empty, like this one?"

"How do I know? If they're unmarked, there's no record."

"Then those traces don't mean anything, do they? We might dig all eight and find every one a dud."

I nodded. "We surely might, Boyce."

He looked at me alertly. "And?"

"And that's not the worst part of it. At least this trace was a real tunnel. I've taken parties out who would've gone mad with joy to open even a breached tunnel, after a couple of weeks of digging up dikes and intrusions. It's perfectly possible all seven of those others are nothing at all. Don't knock it, Boyce. At least you got some action for your money."

He brushed that off. "You picked this spot, Walthers. Did you know what you were doing?"

Did I? The only way to prove that to him would be to find a live one, of course. I could have told him about the months of studying records from the first landings on. I could have mentioned how much trouble I went to, and how many regulations I broke to get a look at the military survey reports, or how far I'd traveled to talk to the Defense crews who'd been on some of the early digs. I might have let him know how hard it had been to locate old Joro-lemon Hegramet, now teaching exotic archaeology back in Tennes-see; but all I said was, "The fact that we found one tunnel shows that I know my business. That's all you paid for. It's up to you whether we keep looking or not."

He gazed at his thumbnail, considering.

"Buck up, Boyce," Dorrie said cheerfully. "Look at the other chances we've still got—and even if we miss, it'll still be fun telling everybody about it back in Cincinnati."

He didn't even look at her, just said, "Isn't there a way of telling whether or not a tunnel has been breached without going inside?"

"Sure. You can tell by tapping the outside shell. You can hear the difference in the sound."

"But you have to dig down to it first?"

"Right."

We left it at that. I got back into my heatsuit to strip away the now useless igloo so that we could move the drills.

I didn't really want to discuss it anymore, because I didn't want him to ask me a question I might have to lie about. I try the best I can to stick to the truth, because it's easier to remember what you've said that way.

On the other hand, I'm not fanatic about it. I don't see that it's any of my business to correct a mistaken impression. For instance, obviously Cochenour supposed I hadn't bothered to sound the tun-nel before calling them in.

But, of course, I had. That was the first thing I did as soon as the drill got down that far. And when I heard the high-pressure *thunk* it broke my heart. I had to wait a couple of minutes before I could call them to announce that we'd reached the outer casing.

At that time I had not quite faced up to the question of just what I would have done if it had turned out the tunnel was unbreached.

IX

Boyce Cochenour and Dorrie Keefer were maybe the fiftieth or sixtieth party I'd taken on a Heechee dig. I wasn't surprised that they were willing to work like coolies. I don't care how lazy and bored Terry tourists start out, by the time they actually come close to finding something that once belonged to an almost completely unknown alien race, left there when the closest thing to a human being on Earth was a slope-browed, furry little beast whose best trick was killing other beasts by hitting them on the head with antelope bones . . . by then they begin to burn with exploration fever.

So the two of them worked hard. And they drove me hard. And I was as eager as they. Maybe more so as the days went past and I found myself rubbing my right side, just under the short ribs, more and more of the time.

We got a couple looks from the Defense boys. They overflew us in their high-speed airbodies half a dozen times in the first few days. They didn't say much, just formal radio requests for identification. Regulations say that if you find anything you're supposed to report it right away. Over Cochenour's objections I reported finding that first breached tunnel, which surprised them a little, I think.

That's all we had to report.

Site B was a pegmatite dike. The other two fairly bright ones,

that I called D and E, showed nothing at all when we dug—meaning that the sound reflections had probably been caused by nothing more than invisible interfaces in rock or ash or gravel.

I vetoed trying to dig Site C, the best looking of the bunch.

Cochenour gave me a hell of an argument about it, but I held out. The military were still looking in on us every now and then, and I didn't want to get any closer to their perimeter than we already were. I said maybe, if we didn't have any luck elsewhere, we could sneak back to C for a quick dig before returning to the Spindle, and we left it at that.

We lifted the airbody, moved to a new position, and set out a new pattern of probes.

By the end of the second week we had dug nine times and come up empty all nine. We were getting low on igloos and probe percussers. We'd run out of tolerance for each other completely.

Cochenour had turned sullen and savage. I hadn't planned on being best buddies with the man when I first met him, but I hadn't expected him to be as bad company as that. I didn't think he had any right to take it so hard, because it was obviously only a game with him. With all his fortune, the extra money he might pick up by discovering some new Heechee artifacts couldn't have meant much—just extra points on a scorepad—but he was playing for blood.

I wasn't particularly gracious myself, for that matter. The plain fact was that the pills from the Quackery weren't helping as much as they should. My mouth tasted as though rats had nested in it, I was getting headaches, and every once in a while I'd be woozy enough to knock things over.

See, the thing about the liver is that it sort of regulates your internal diet. It filters out poisons. It converts some of the carbohydrates into other carbohydrates that you can use. It patches together amino acids into proteins. If it isn't working, you die.

The doctor had been all over it with me. Maze-rats get liver trouble a lot; it comes when you save yourself a little trouble by letting your internal suit pressure build up—it sort of compresses the gas in your gut and squeezes the liver. He'd showed me pictures. I could visualize what was going on in my insides, with the mahogany-red liver cells dying and being replaced by clusters of fat and yellowish stuff. It was an ugly picture. The ugliest part was that there wasn't anything I could do about it. Only go on taking pills—and they wouldn't work much longer. I counted the days to byebye, liver, hello, hepatic failure.

So we were a bad bunch. I was being a bastard because I was beginning to feel sick and desperate. Cochenour was being a bastard because that was his nature. The only decent human being aboard was the girl.

Dorrie did her best, she really did. She was sometimes sweet (and often even pretty), and she was always ready to meet the power people, Cochenour and me, more than halfway.

It was obvious that it was tough on her. Dorotha Keefer was only a kid. No matter how grown-up she acted, she just hadn't been alive long enough to grow defenses against concentrated meanness. Add in the fact that we were all beginning to hate the sight and sound and smell of each other (and in an airbody you get to know a lot about how people smell), and there wasn't much joy in this skylarking tour of Venus for Dorrie Keefer.

Or for any of us . . . especially after I broke the news that we were down to our last igloo.

Cochenour cleared his throat. It wasn't a polite sound. It was the beginning of a war cry. He sounded like a fighter-plane jockey blowing the covers off his guns in preparation for combat, and Dorrie tried to head him off with a diversion. "Audee," she said brightly, "do you know what I think we could do? We could go back to that Site C, the one that looked good near the military reservation."

It was the wrong diversion. I shook my head. "No."

"What the hell do you mean, 'No'?" Cochenour rumbled, revving up for battle.

"What I said. No. It's too close to the Defense guys. If there's a tunnel, it will run right onto the reservation, and they'll come down on us." I tried to be persuasive. "That's a desperation trick, and I'm not that desperate."

"Walthers," he snarled, "you'll be desperate if I tell you to be desperate. I can still stop payment on that check."

I corrected him. "No, you can't. The union won't let you. The regulations are very clear about that. You pay up unless I disobey a lawful request. What you want isn't lawful. Going inside the military reservation is extremely against the law."

He shifted over to cold war. "No," he said softly. "You're wrong about that. It's only against the law if a court says it is, after we do it. You're only right if your lawyers are smarter than my lawyer. Honestly, Walthers, they won't be. I pay my lawyers to be the smartest there are."

I was not in a good bargaining position. It wasn't just that what Cochenour said was true enough. He had help from a very powerful ally. My liver was on his side. I certainly could not spare time for arbitration, because without the transplant his payment was going to buy I wouldn't live that long.

Dorrie had been listening with her birdlike air of friendly interest. She got between us. "Well, then, how about this? We just got to where we are now. Why don't we wait and see what the probes show? Maybe we'll hit something even better than that Site C—"

"There isn't going to be anything good here," he said without taking his eyes off me.

"Why, Boyce, how do you know that? We haven't even finished the soundings."

He said, "Look, Dorotha, listen close this one time and then shut up. Walthers is playing games with me. Do you see where we just put down?"

He brushed past me and tapped out the command for a full map display, which somewhat surprised me. I hadn't known he knew how. The charts sprang up. They showed the virtual images of our position and of the shafts we'd already cut, and the great irregular border of the military reservation—all overlaid on the plot of mascons and navigation aids.

"Do you see the picture? We're not even in the high-density mass-concentration areas now. Isn't that true, Walthers? Are you saying we've tried all the good locations around here and come up dry?"

"No," I said. "That is, you're partly right, Mr. Cochenour. Only partly; I'm not playing any games with you. This site is a good possibility. You can see it on the map. It's true that we're not right over any mascon, but we're right between those two right there, that are pretty close together. That's a good sign. Sometimes you find a dig that connects two complexes, and it has happened that the connecting passage was closer to the surface there than any other part of the system. I can't guarantee that we'll hit anything here. But it's worth a gamble."

"It's just damn unlikely, right?"

"Well, no more unlikely than anywhere else. I told you a week ago, you got your money's worth the first day, just finding any Heechee tunnel at all. Even a spoiled one. There are maze-rats in the Spindle who went five years without seeing that much." I thought for a minute. "I'll make a deal with you," I offered.

"I'm listening."

"We're already on the ground here. There's at least a chance we can hit something. Let's try. We'll deploy the probes and see what they turn up. If we get a good trace we'll dig it. If not . . . well, then I'll think about going back to Site C."

"*Think* about it!" he roared.

"Don't push me, Cochenour. You don't know what you're getting into. The military reservation is not to be fooled with. Those boys shoot first and ask later, and there aren't any policemen around to holler for help."

"I don't know," he said after a moment's glowering thought.

"No," I told him, "you don't, Mr. Cochenour. I do. That's what you're paying me for."

He nodded. "Yes, you probably do know, Walthers, but whether you're telling me the truth about what you know is another question. Hegramet never said anything about digging between mascons."

And then he looked at me with a completely opaque expression, waiting to see whether I would catch him up on what he'd just said.

I didn't respond. I gave him an opaque look back. I didn't say a word. I only waited to see what would come next. I was pretty sure it would not be any sort of explanation of how he happened to know Professor Hegramet's name, or what dealings he had had with the greatest Earthside authority on Heechee diggings.

It wasn't.

"Put out your probes," he said at last. "We'll try it your way one more time."

I plopped the probes out, got good penetration on all of them, and started firing the noisemakers. Then I sat watching the first lines of the cast build up on the scan, as though I expected them to carry useful information. They weren't going to for quite a while, but I wanted to think privately for a bit.

Cochenour needed to be thought about. He hadn't come to Venus just for the ride. He had planned to dig for Heechee tunnels before he ever left the Earth. He had gone to the trouble of briefing himself even on the instruments he would encounter in an airbody.

My sales talk about Heechee treasures had been wasted on a customer whose mind had been made up to buy at least half a year earlier and tens of millions of miles away.

I understood all that. But the more I understood, the more I saw that I didn't understand. I wished I could slip Cochenour a couple of bucks and send him off to the games parlors for a while, so I could talk privately to the girl. Unfortunately there wasn't anywhere to send him. I forced a yawn, complained about the boredom of waiting for the probe traces to build up, and suggested we all take a nap. Not that I would have been real confident he would be the one to turn in—but he didn't even listen. All I got out of that ploy was an offer from Dorrie to watch the screen and wake me up if anything interesting developed.

So I said the hell with it and turned in myself.

I didn't sleep well, because while I was lying there, waiting for sleep to happen, it gave me time to notice how truly lousy I was beginning to feel, and in how many different ways. There was a sort of permanent taste of bile in the back of my mouth—not so much as though I wanted to throw up as it was as though I just had. My head ached. My eyes were getting woozy; I was beginning to see ghost images wandering fuzzily around my field of vision.

I roused myself to take a couple of my pills. I didn't count the ones that were left. I didn't want to know.

I set my private wake-up for three hours, thinking maybe that would give Cochenour time to get sleepy and turn in, leaving Dorrie perhaps up and maybe feeling conversational. But when I woke up there was the wide-awake old man, cooking himself a herb omelet with the last of our sterile eggs. "You were right, Walthers," he grinned. "I was sleepy, at that. So I had a nice little one-hour nap. Ready for anything now. Want some eggs?"

Actually I did want them. A lot. But of course I didn't dare eat them, so I glumly swallowed the nutritious and very unsatisfying stuff the diet department of the Quackery allowed me to have and watched him stuff himself. It was unfair that a man of ninety could be so healthy that he didn't have to think about his digestion, while I was—

Well, there wasn't any profit in that kind of thinking. I offered to play some music to pass the time. Dorrie picked *Swan Lake*, and I started it up.

And then I had an idea. I headed for the tool lockers. They didn't really need checking. The auger heads were close to time for replacement, but I wasn't going to replace them; we were running low on spares. The thing about the tool lockers was that they were about as far from the galley as you could get and still be inside the airbody.

I hoped Dorrie would follow me. And she did.

"Need any help, Audee?"

"Glad to have it," I told her. "Here, hold these for me. Don't get the grease on your clothes." I didn't expect her to ask why they had to be held. She didn't. She only laughed at the idea of getting grease on her clothes.

"I don't think I'd even notice a little extra grease, dirty as I am. I guess we'll all be glad to get back to civilization."

Cochenour was frowning over the probe and paying no attention. I said, "Which kind of civilization do you mean? The Spindle, or all the way back to Earth?"

What I had in mind was to start her talking about Earth, but she went the other way. "Oh, the Spindle," she said. "I never dreamed I'd get to this planet, Audee! I loved it. I thought it was fascinating the way everybody got along together, and we really didn't see much of it. Especially the people, like that Indian fellow who ran the restaurant. The cashier was his wife, wasn't she?"

"She was one of them, yes. She's Vastra's number-one wife. The waitress was number three, and he has another one at home with the kids. There are five kids, all three wives involved." But I wanted to turn the conversation around, so I said, "It's pretty much the same as on Earth. Vastra would be running a tourist trap in Benares if he wasn't running one here, and he wouldn't be here if he hadn't shipped out with the military and terminated here. I guess if I weren't on Venus I'd be guiding in Texas. If there's any open country left to guide hunters in—maybe up along the Canadian River. How about you?"

All the time I was picking up the same four or five tools, studying the serial numbers and putting them back. She didn't notice.

"How do you mean?"

"Well, what did you do on Earth, before you came here?"

"Oh, I worked in Boyce's office for a while."

That was encouraging. Maybe she'd remember something about his connection with Professor Hegramet. "What were you, a secretary?"

She gave me an unfriendly look. "Something like that," she said.

Then I was embarrassed. She thought I was prying—I was, of course, but I wasn't looking for sordid details about how a pretty

young thing like her allowed herself to be seduced into being bed-mate for a dirty old man. Not least because Cochenour, old though he was and nasty as he might be when he chose, was also obviously a pretty powerfully attractive figure to women. I said, trying to be placating, "It's none of my business, of course."

"No," she said, "it isn't." And then she said, "What's that?"

That was an incoming call on the radio, that's what that was.

"So answer it," Cochenour snarled from across the airbody, looking up from his eggs.

I was glad enough for the interruption. The call was voice-only, which surprised me a little. I kept it that way. In fact, I took the call on the earjack, since it is my nature to be cautious about some things. Anyway, there isn't much privacy in an airbody, and I want what little crumbs of it I can find.

THE GATEWAY TRIP

It was the base calling, a Communications sergeant I knew
named Littleknees. I signed in irritably, watching Dorrie go back to
sit protectively with Boyce Cochenour.

"A private word for you, Audee," said Sergeant Littleknees. "Is
your sahib lurking about?"

Littleknees and I had exchanged radio chatter for a long time.
There was something about the bright cheeriness of the tone that
bothered me. I turned my back on Cochenour. I knew he was listening—but only to my side of the conversation, of course, because
of the earjack. "In the area but not tuned in at present," I said.
"What have you got for me?"

"Just a little news bulletin," the sergeant purred. "It came in
over the synsat a couple of minutes ago, information only as far as
we were concerned. That means we don't have to do anything about
it, but maybe you do, honey."

"Standing by," I said, studying the plastic housing of the radio.

The sergeant chuckled. "Your sahib's charter captain would like
to have a word with him when found. It's kind of urgent, 'cause
the captain is righteously pissed off."

"Yes, Base," I said. "Your signals received, strength ten."

Sergeant Amanda Littleknees made an amused noise again, but
this time it wasn't a chuckle. It was a downright giggle. "The thing
is," she said, "his check for the charter fee for the *Yuri Gagarin*
went bouncy-bouncy. Do you want to know what the bank said?
You'd never guess. 'Insufficient funds,' that's what they said."

The pain under my right lower ribs was permanent, but right
then it seemed to get a lot worse. I gritted my teeth. "Ah, Sergeant
Littleknees," I croaked. "Can you verify that estimate?"

"Sorry, honey," she buzzed in my ear, "but there's no doubt
in the world. The captain got a credit report on your Boyce Cochenour fellow, and it turned up n.g. When your customer gets back
to the Spindle there'll be a warrant waiting for him."

"Thank you for the synoptic estimate," I said hollowly. "I will
verify departure time before we take off."

80

And I turned off the radio and gazed at my rich billionaire client.

"What the hell's the matter with you, Walthers?" he growled.

But I wasn't hearing his voice. I was only hearing what my happy sawbones at the Quackery had told me. The equations were unforgettable. Cash = new liver + happy survival. No cash = total hepatic failure + death. And my cash supply had just dried up.

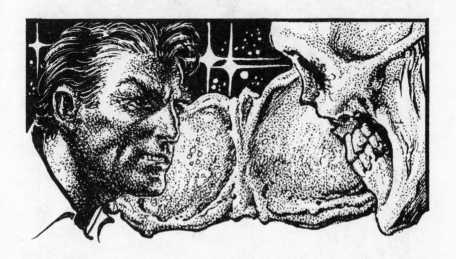

X

When you get a really big piece of news you have to let it trickle through your system and get thoroughly absorbed before you do anything about it. It isn't a matter of seeing the implications. I saw those right away, you bet I did. It's a matter of letting the system reach equilibrium.

So I puttered for a few minutes. I listened to Tchaikovsky's swan hunters tooling up to meet the queen. I made sure the radio switch was off so as not to waste power. I checked the synoptic plot the thumpers were building up.

It would have been nice if there had been something wonderful beginning to show on it, but, the way things were going, there wouldn't be, of course. There wasn't. A few pale echoes were beginning to form. But nothing with the shape of a Heechee tunnel, and nothing very bright. The data were still coming in, but I knew there was no way for those feeble plots to develop into the mother lode that could save us all, even crooked, dead-broke, bastard Cochenour.

I even looked out at as much of the sky as I could manage through the windows, to see how the weather was. It didn't matter, but some of the big white calomel clouds were scudding among the purples and yellows of the other mercury halides; the sun was getting ready to rise in the west.

It was beautiful, and I hated it.

Cochenour had put away the last of his omelet and was watching me thoughtfully. So was Dorrie, back at the parts rack, once again holding the augers in their grease-paper wrap. I grinned at her. "Pretty," I said, referring to the music. The Auckland Philharmonic was just getting to the part where the baby swans come out arm in arm and do a fast, bouncy pas de quatre across the stage. It has always been one of my favorite parts of *Swan Lake* ... but not now.

"We'll listen to the rest of it later," I said, and switched the player off.

Cochenour snapped, "All right, Walthers. What's going on?"

I sat down on an empty igloo pack and lit a cigarette, because one of the adjustments my internal system had made was to calculate that we didn't need to worry much about coddling our oxygen supply anymore. "There are some questions that have been bothering me, Cochenour. For one, how did you happen to get in touch with Professor Hegramet?"

He grinned and relaxed. "Oh, is that all that's on your mind? No reason you shouldn't know that. I did a lot of checking on Venus before I came out here—why not?"

"No reason, except you let me think you didn't know a thing."

Cochenour shrugged. "If you had any brains at all you'd know I didn't get rich by being stupid. You think I'd travel umpty-million miles without knowing what I was going to find when I got here?"

"No, you wouldn't, but you did your best to make me think you would. No matter. So you went looking for somebody who could point you to whatever was worth stealing on Venus, and then that person steered you to Hegramet. Then what? Did Hegramet tell you that I was dumb enough to be your boy?"

Cochenour wasn't quite as relaxed, but he hadn't turned aggressive, either. He said mildly, "Hegramet did mention your name, yes. He told me you were as good a guide as any if I wanted to look for a virgin tunnel. Then he answered a lot of questions for me about the Heechee and so on. So, yes, I knew who you were. If you hadn't come to us I would have come to you; you just saved me the trouble."

I said, feeling a little surprise as I said it, "You know, I think you're telling me the truth. Except that you left out one thing."

"Which was?"

"It wasn't the fun of making more money that you were after, was it? It was just money, right? Money that you needed pretty badly." I turned to Dorotha, standing frozen with the augers in her hands. "How about it, Dorrie? Did you know the old man was broke?"

It wasn't too smart of me to put it to her like that. I saw what she was about to do just before she did it, and jumped off the igloo crate. I was a little too late. She dropped the augers before I could take them away from her, but fortunately they landed flat and the blades weren't chipped. I picked them up and put them away.

She had answered the question well enough.

"I see he didn't tell you about that," I said. "That's tough on you, doll. His check to the captain of the *Gagarin* is still bouncing, and I would imagine the one he gave me isn't going to be much better. I hope you got it all in fur and jewels, Dorrie. My advice to you is to hide them before the creditors want them back."

She didn't even look at me. She was only looking at Cochenour, whose expression was all the confirmation she needed.

I don't know what I expected from her, rage or reproaches or tears. What she did was whisper, "Oh, Boyce, dear, I'm so sorry." And she went over and put her arms around him.

I turned my back on them, because I wasn't enjoying looking at the way he was. The strapping ninety-year-old buck on Full Medical had turned into a defeated old man. For the first time since he'd walked cockily into the Spindle, he looked all of his age and maybe a little bit more. The mouth was half-open, trembling; the straight back was stooped; the bright blue eyes were watering. Dorrie stroked him and crooned to him, looking at me with an expression filled with pain.

It had never occurred to me that she might really care about the guy.

I turned and studied the synoptic web again, for lack of anything better to do. It was about as clear as it was ever going to get, and it was empty. We had a little overlap from one of our previous soundings, so I could tell that the interesting-looking scratches on one edge were nothing to get excited about. We'd checked them out already. They were only ghosts.

There was no instant salvation waiting for us there.

Curiously, I felt kind of relaxed. There is something tranquilizing about the realization that you don't have anything much to lose anymore. It puts things in a different perspective.

I don't mean to say that I had given up. There were still things I could do. They didn't have much to do with prolonging my life anymore—that was one of the things I had had to readjust to—but then the taste in my mouth and the pain in my gut weren't letting me enjoy life very much anyway.

One thing I could do was to write good old Audee Walthers off. Since only a miracle could keep me from that famous total hepatic collapse in a week or two, I could accept the fact that I wasn't going to be alive much longer. So I could use what time I had left for something else.

What else? Well, Dorrie was not a bad kid. I could fly the air-body back to the Spindle, turn Cochenour over to the gendarmes, and spend my last couple of walking-around days introducing Dorrie to the people who could help her. Vastra or BeeGee would be willing to give her some kind of a start, maybe. She might not even have to go into prostitution or the rackets. The high season wasn't all that far off, and she had the kind of personality that might make a success out of a little booth of prayer fans and Heechee lucky pieces for the Terry tourists.

Maybe that wasn't much, from anyone's point of view. But the captain of the *Gagarin* was surely not going to fly her back to Cincinnati for nothing, and scrounging in the Spindle beat starving. Somewhat.

Then maybe I didn't really have to give up on myself, even? I thought about that for a bit. I could fling myself on the mercy of the Quackery. Conceivably they might let me have a new liver on credit. Why not?

There was one good reason why not; namely, they never had.

Or I could open the two-fuel valves and let them mix for ten minutes or so before hitting the igniter. The explosion wouldn't leave much of the airbody—or of us—and nothing at all of our various problems.

Or—

I sighed. "Oh, hell," I said. "Buck up, Cochenour. We're not dead yet."

He looked at me for a moment to see if I'd gone crazy. Then he patted Dorrie's shoulder and pushed her away, gently enough. "I will be, soon enough. I'm sorry about all this, Dorotha. And I'm sorry about your check, Walthers; I expect you needed the money."

"You have no idea."

He said with some difficulty, "Do you want me to try to explain?"

"I don't see that it makes any difference—but, yes," I admitted, "out of curiosity I do."

It didn't take him long. Once he started, he was succinct and clear and he didn't leave any important things out—although actually I could have guessed most of it. (But hadn't. Hindsight is so much better.)

The basic thing is that a man Cochenour's age has to be one of two things. Either he's very, very rich, or he's dead. Cochenour's trouble was that he was only *quite* rich. He'd done his best to keep all his industries going with a depleted cash flow of what was left after he siphoned off the costs of transplants and treatments, calciphylaxis and prosthesis, protein regeneration here, cholesterol flushing there, a million for this, a hundred grand a month for that . . . oh, it went fast enough. I could see that. "You just don't know," he said, not pitifully, just stating a fact, "what it takes to keep a hundred-year-old man alive until you try it."

Oh, don't I just, I said, but not out loud. I let him go on with the story of how the minority stockholders were getting inquisitive and the federal inspectors were closing in . . . and so he skipped Earth to make his fortune all over again on Venus.

But I wasn't listening attentively anymore by the time he got to the end of it. I didn't even pick up on the fact that he'd been lying about his age—imagine that vanity! Thinking it was better to say he was ninety!

I had more important things to do than make Cochenour squirm anymore. Instead of listening I was writing on the back of a navigation form. When I was finished, I passed it over to Cochenour. "Sign it," I said.

"What is it?"

"Does it matter? You don't have any choice that I can see. But what it is is a release from the all-rights section of our charter agreement. You acknowledge that the charter is void, that you have no claim, that your check was rubber, and that you voluntarily waive your ownership of anything we might find in my favor."

He was frowning. "What's this bit at the end?"

"That's where I agree to give you ten percent of my share of the profits on anything we find, *if* we do find anything worth money."

"That's charity," he said, looking up at me. But he was already signing. "I don't mind taking a little charity, especially since, as you point out, I don't have any choice. But I can read that synoptic web over there as well as you can, Walthers. There's nothing on it to find."

"No, there isn't," I agreed, folding the paper and putting it in my pocket. "That trace is as bare as your bank account. But we're not going to dig there. What we're going to do is go back and dig Site C."

I lit another cigarette—lung cancer was the least of my worries just then—and thought for a minute while they waited, watching me. I was wondering how much to tell them of what I had spent five years finding out and figuring out, schooling myself not even to hint at it to anyone else. I was sure in my mind that nothing I said would make a difference anymore. Even so, the habits of years were strong. The words didn't want to say themselves.

It took a real effort for me to make myself start.

"You remember Subhash Vastra, the fellow who ran the trap where I met you? Sub came to Venus during his hitch with the military. He was a weapons specialist. There isn't any civilian career for a weapons specialist, especially on Venus, so he went into the café business with most of his termination bonus when he got out. Then he sent for his wives with the rest of it. But he was supposed to be pretty good at weaponry while he was in the service."

"What are you saying, Audee?" Dorrie asked. "I never heard of any Heechee weapons."

"No. Nobody has ever found a Heechee weapon. But Sub thinks they found targets."

It was actually physically difficult for me to force my lips to speak the next part, but I got it out. "Anyway, Sub Vastra thought they were targets. He said the higher brass didn't believe him, and I think the matter has been pigeonholed on the reservation now. But what they found was triangular pieces of Heechee wall material—that blue, light-emitting stuff they lined the tunnels with. There were dozens of the things. They all had a pattern of radiating lines; Sub says they looked like targets to him. And they had been drilled through, by something that left the holes as chalky as talcum powder. Do you happen to know of anything that will do that to Heechee wall material?"

Dorrie was about to say she didn't, but Cochenour said it for her. "That's impossible," he said flatly.

"Right, that's what the brass told Sub Vastra. They decided that the holes were made in the process of fabrication, for some Heechee purpose we'll never know. Vastra doesn't believe that. Vastra says he figured they were just about the same as the paper targets soldiers use on the firing range. The holes weren't all in the same place. The lines looked to him like scoring markers. That's all the evidence there is that Vastra's right. Not proof. Even Vastra doesn't think it's proof. But it's evidence, anyway."

"And you think you can find the gun that made those holes where we located Site C?" Cochenour asked.

I hesitated. "I wouldn't put it that strongly. Call it a hope. Maybe even a very outside hope. But there's one more thing.

"These targets, or whatever they are, were turned up by a prospector nearly forty years ago. There wasn't any military reservation then. He turned them in to see if anybody would buy them, and nobody was very interested. Then he went out looking for something better, and after a while he got himself killed. That happened a lot in those days. No one paid much attention to the things until some military types got a look at them, and then somebody had the same idea Vastra had years later. So they got serious. They identified the site where he'd reported finding them, near the South Pole. They staked off everything for a thousand kilometers around and labeled it off limits: that's how come the reservation is where it is. And they dug and dug. They turned up about a dozen Heechee tunnels, but most of them were bare and the rest were cracked and spoiled. They didn't find anything like a weapon."

"Then there's nothing there," Cochenour growled, looking perplexed.

"There's nothing they found," I corrected him. "Remember, this was forty years ago."

Cochenour looked at me, puzzled, then his expression cleared. "Oh," he said. "The location of the find."

I nodded. "That's right. In those days prospectors lied a lot—if they found something good, they didn't want other people horning in. So he gave the wrong location for his tunnel. At that time, he was shacked up with a young lady who later married a man named Allemang—her son, Booker, is a friend of mine. BeeGee. You met him. And he had a map."

Cochenour was looking openly skeptical now. "Oh, right," he said sourly. "The famous treasure map. And he just gave it to you out of friendship."

"He sold it to me," I said.

"Wonderful. How many copies do you suppose he sold other suckers."

"Not many." I didn't blame Cochenour for doubting the story, but he was rubbing me the wrong way. "I got him right when he came back from trying to find it on his own; he didn't have time to try anybody else." I saw Cochenour opening his mouth and went ahead to forestall him. "No, he didn't find anything. Yes, he thought he followed the map. That's why I didn't have to pay much. But you see I think he missed the right place. The right location on the map, as near as I can figure—the navigation systems then weren't what they are now—is right about where we set down the first time, give or take some. I saw some digging marks a couple of times. I think they were pretty old." I slipped the little private magnetofiche out of my pocket while I was talking and put it into the virtual map display. It showed one central mark, an orange **X**. "That's where I think we might find the right tunnel, somewhere near that **X**. And, as you can see, that's pretty close to our old Site C."

Silence for a minute. I listened to the distant outside rumble of the winds, waiting for the others to say something.

Dorrie was looking troubled. "I don't know if I like the idea of trying to find a new weapon," she said. "It's—it's like bringing back the bad old days."

I shrugged.

Cochenour was beginning to look more like himself again. "The point isn't whether we really want to find a weapon, is it? The point is that we want to find an untapped Heechee dig for whatever's in

91

it. But the soldiers think there *might* be a weapon somewhere around, so they aren't going to let us dig, right?"

"Not 'think.' 'Thought.' I doubt any of them believe it any-more."

"All the same, they'll shoot us first and ask questions later. Isn't that what you said?"

"That's what I said. Nobody's ever allowed on the reservation without clearance. Not because of Heechee weapons; they've got lots of their own stuff there that they don't want people seeing."

He nodded. "So how do you propose to get around that little problem?" he asked.

If I were a completely truthful man I probably should have said that I wasn't sure I would get around it. Looked at honestly, the odds were pretty poor. We could easily get caught and, although I didn't think it was certain, very possibly shot.

But we had so little to lose, Cochenour and I at least, that I didn't think that was important enough to mention. I just said, "We'll try to fool them. We'll send the airbody off. You and I will stay behind to do the digging. If they think we're gone, they won't be keeping us under surveillance. All we'd have to worry about is being picked up on a routine perimeter patrol, but they're fairly careless about those. I hope."

"Audee!" the girl cried. "What are you talking about? If you and Boyce stay here, who's going to run the airbody? *I* can't!"

"No," I agreed, "you can't, or not very well—even after I give you a couple of lessons. But you can let the thing fly itself. Oh, you'll waste fuel, and you'll get bounced around a lot. But you'll get where you're going on autopilot. It'll even land you on its own."

"You haven't landed that way," Cochenour pointed out.

"I didn't say it would be a *good* landing. You'd better be strapped in." What it would be, of course, was something more like a con-trolled crash; I closed my mind to the thought of what an autopilot landing might do to my one and only airbody. Dorrie would sur-vive it, though. Ninety-nine chances out of a hundred.

"Then what do I do?" Dorrie asked.

There were big holes in my plan at that point, too, but I closed my mind to them, as well. "That depends on where you go. I think the best plan would be for you to head right back to the Spindle."

"And leave you here?" she demanded, looking suddenly rebellious.

"Not permanently. In the Spindle you look up my friend BeeGee Allemang and tell him what's been going on. He'll want a share, naturally, but that's all right; we can give him twenty-five percent, and he'll be happy with that. I'll give you a note for him with all the coordinates and so on, and he'll fly the airbody right back here to pick us up. Say twenty-four hours later."

"Can we do all that in a day?" Cochenour wanted to know.

"Sure we can. We have to."

"And what if Dorrie can't find him, or he gets lost, or something?"

"She'll find him, and he won't get lost. Of course," I admitted, "there's always the possibility of some 'something.' We have a little margin for error. We can take tanks for extra air and power—we should be all right for as much as forty-eight hours. No more than that. It'll be cutting it very close, but that's plenty of time, I think. If he's late, of course, we're in trouble; but he won't be. What I really worry about is that we'll dig that tunnel and it'll be no good. Then we've wasted our time. But if we do find anything . . ." I left it there.

"Sounds pretty chancy," Cochenour observed, but he was looking at Dorrie, not at me. She shrugged.

"I didn't say it was a guarantee," I told him. "I only said it was a chance."

I was beginning to think very well of Dorotha Keefer. She was a pretty nice person, considering her age and circumstances, and smart and strong, too. But one thing she lacked was self-confidence.

93

She had just never been trained to it. She had been getting it as a prosthesis—from Cochenour most recently, I supposed, before that maybe whoever preceded Cochenour in her life—at her age, perhaps that had been her father. She had the air of somebody who'd been surrounded by dominating people for a long time.

That was the biggest problem, persuading Dorrie that she could do her part. "It won't work," she kept saying, as I went over the controls with her. "I'm sorry. It isn't that I don't want to help. I do, but I can't. It just won't work."

Well, it would have.

Or at least, I think it would have. In the event, we never got to try the plan out.

Between us, Cochenour and I finally got Dorrie to agree to give it a whirl. We packed up what little salvageable gear we'd put out-side. We flew back to the ravine, landed, and began to set up for a dig. But I was feeling poorly—thick, headachy, clumsy—and I sup-pose Cochenour had his own problems, though I must admit he didn't complain. Between the two of us we managed to catch the casing of the drill in the exit port while we were off-loading it.

And, while I was jockeying it one way from above, Cochenour pulled the other way from beneath . . . and the whole hard, heavy thing came right down on top of him.

It didn't kill him. It just gouged his suit and broke his leg and knocked him unconscious, and that took care of any possibility of having him to help me dig Site C.

XI

The first thing I did was to check the drill to make sure it wasn't damaged. It wasn't. The second was to manhandle Cochenour back into the airbody lock.

That took about everything I had, with the combined weight

of our suits and bodies, getting the drill out of the way, and my general physical condition. But I managed it.

Dorrie was great. No hysteria, no foolish questions. We got him out of his heatsuit and looked him over.

The suit leg had been ruptured through eight or ten plies, but there had been enough left to keep the air out, if not all the pressure. He was alive. Unconscious, all right, but breathing. The leg fracture was compounded, with bone showing through the bleeding flesh. He was bleeding, too, from the mouth and nose, and he had vomited inside his helmet.

All in all, he was about the worst-looking hundred-or-whatever-year-old man you'll ever see—live one, anyway. But he didn't seem to have taken enough heat to cook his brain. His heart was still going—well, I mean whoever's heart it had been in the first place was still going. It was a good investment, because it was pumping right along. We put compresses on everything we could find, and most of the bleeding stopped by itself, except from the nasty business on his leg.

For that we needed more expert help. Dorrie called the military reservation for me. She got Amanda Littleknees and was put right through to the base surgeon, Colonel Eve Marcuse. Dr. Marcuse was a friend of my own Quackery fellow; I'd met her once or twice, and she was good about telling me what to do.

At first Colonel Marcuse wanted me to pack up and bring Cochenour right over. I vetoed that. I gave her satisfactory reasons—I wasn't in shape to pilot, and it would be a rough ride for Cochenour. I certainly didn't give her the real reason, namely that I didn't want to get into the reservation and have to explain my way out of it again. So instead she gave me step-by-step instructions on what to do with the casualty.

They were easy enough to follow, and I did all she commanded: reduced the fracture, packed the gash, stuck Cochenour with broad-spectrum antibiotics, closed the wound with surgical Velcro and meat glue, sprayed a bandage all around, and poured on a cast. It

depleted our first-aid supplies pretty thoroughly and took about an hour of our time. Cochenour would have come to while we were doing it, except that I had also given him a sleepy needle.

Then he was stable enough. From then on it was just a matter of taking pulse and respiration and blood-pressure readings to satisfy the surgeon, and promising to get him back to the Spindle pretty soon. When Dr. Marcuse was through, still annoyed with me for not bringing Cochenour in for her to play with—I think she was fascinated by the idea of cutting into a man composed almost entirely of other people's parts—Sergeant Littleknees came back on the circuit.

I could tell what was on her mind. "Uh, honey? How did it happen, exactly?"

"A great big Heechee came exactly up out of the ground and bit him exactly on the leg," I told her. "I know what you're thinking. You've got an evil mind. It was just an accident."

"Of course it was," she said. "I just wanted you to know that I don't blame you a bit." And she signed off.

Dorrie was cleaning the old man off as best she could—pretty profligate with our spare sheets and towels, I thought, considering that my airbody didn't carry a washing machine aboard. I left her to it while I made myself some coffee, lit another cigarette, and sat and thought up another plan.

By the time Dorrie had done what she could for Cochenour, then cleaned up the worst of the mess, then begun such remaining important tasks as the repair of her eye makeup, I had thought up a dandy.

As the first step, I gave Cochenour a wake-up needle.

Dorrie patted him and talked to him while he got his bearings. She was not a girl who carried a grudge. On the other hand, I did, a little. I wasn't as tender as she. As soon as he seemed coherent I got him up, to try out his muscles—a lot faster than he really wanted to. His expression told me that they all ached. They worked all right, though, and he could stump around on the cast.

He was even able to grin. "Old bones," he said. "I knew I should have gone for another recalciphylaxis. That's what happens when you try to save a buck."

He sat down heavily, wincing, the leg stuck out in front of him. He wrinkled his nose as he smelled himself. "Sorry to have messed up your nice clean airbody," he added.

"It's been messed up worse. You want to finish cleaning yourself up?"

He looked surprised. "Well, I guess I'd better, pretty soon—"

"Do it now. I want to talk to you both."

He didn't argue. He just stuck out his hand, and Dorrie took it. With her help he stumped, half-hopping, toward the clean-up. Actually Dorrie had already done the worst of the job of getting him clean before he woke up, but he splashed a little water on his face and swished some around in his mouth. He was pretty well recovered when he turned around to look at me.

"All right, Walthers, what is it? Do we give up and go back now?"

"No," I said. "We'll do it a different way."

"He can't, Audee!" Dorrie cried. "Look at him. And the condition his suit is in, he couldn't last outside an hour, much less help you dig."

"I know that, so we'll have to change the plan. I'll dig by myself. The two of you will slope off in the airbody."

"Oh, brave heroic man," Cochenour said flatly. "Are you *crazy*? Who are you kidding? That's a two-man job."

"I did the first one by myself, Cochenour."

"And came into the airbody to cool off every little while. Sure. That's a whole other thing."

I hesitated. "It'll be harder," I admitted. "Not impossible. Lone prospectors have dug out tunnels before, though the problems were a little different. I know it'll be a rough forty-eight hours for me, but we'll have to try it—there isn't any alternative."

"Wrong," Cochenour said. He patted Dorrie's rump. "Solid muscle, that girl is. She isn't big, but she's healthy. Takes after her grandmother. Don't argue, Walthers. Just think a little bit. I'll fly the airbody; she'll stick around to help you. The job is as safe for Dorrie as it is for you; and with two of you to spell each other there's a chance you might make it before you pass out from heat prostration. What's the chance by yourself? Any chance at all?"

I didn't answer the last part. For some reason, his attitude put me in a bad temper. "You talk as though she didn't have anything to say about it."

"Well," Dorrie said, sweetly enough, "come to that, so do you, Audee. Boyce is right. I appreciate your being all gallant and trying to make things easy for me, but, honestly, I think you'll need me. I've learned a lot. And if you want the truth, you look a lot worse than I do."

I said, with all the contemptuous command I could get into my voice, "Forget it. We're going to do it my way. You can both help me for an hour or so, while I get set up. Then you're on your way. No arguments. Let's get going."

Well, that made two mistakes.

The first was that we didn't get set up in an hour. It took more than two, and I was sweating—sick, oily sweat—long before we finished. I really felt bad. I was past worrying about the way I felt; I was only a little surprised, and kind of grateful, every time I noticed that my heart was still beating.

Dorrie was as strong and willing as promised. She did more of the muscle work than I did, firing up the igloo and setting the equipment in place, and Cochenour checked over the instruments

and made sure he knew what he had to do to make the airbody fly. He flatly rejected the notion of going back to the Spindle, though; he said he didn't want to risk the extra time, when he could just as easily set down for twenty-four hours a few hundred kilometers away.

Then I took two cups of strong coffee, heavily laced with my private supply of gin, smoked my last cigarette for a while, and put in a call to the military reservation.

Amanda Littleknees was flirtatious but a little puzzled when I told her we were departing the vicinity, no fixed destination; but she didn't argue.

Then Dorrie and I tumbled out of the lock and closed it behind us, leaving Cochenour strapped in the driver's seat.

That was the other mistake I had made. In spite of everything I had said, we did it Cochenour's way after all. I never agreed to it. It just happened that way.

Under the ashy sky Dorrie just stood there for a moment, looking forlorn. But then she grabbed my hand, and the two of us swam through the thick, turbulent air toward the shelter of our last igloo. She had remembered my coaching about the importance of staying out of the jet exhaust. Inside, she flung herself flat and didn't move.

I was less cautious. I couldn't help myself. I had to see. So, as soon as I could judge from the flare that the jets were angled away from us, I stuck my head up and watched Cochenour take off in a sleet of ash.

It wasn't a bad takeoff. In circumstances like that, I define "bad" as total demolition of the airbody and the death or maiming of one or more persons. He avoided that, but as soon as he was out of the slight shelter of the arroyo the gusts caught him and the airbody skittered and slid wildly. It was going to be a rough ride for him, going just the few hundred kilometers north that would take him out of detection range.

I touched Dorrie with my toe, and she struggled to her feet. I slipped the talk cord into the jack on her helmet—radio was out, because of possible eavesdropping from the perimeter patrols that we wouldn't be able to see.

"Have you changed your mind yet?" I asked.

It was a fairly obnoxious question, but she took it nicely. She giggled. I could tell that because we were faceplate to faceplate, and I could see her face shadowed inside the helmet. But I couldn't hear what she was saying until she remembered to nudge her voice switch, and then what I heard was, ". . . romantic, just the two of us."

Well, we didn't have time for that kind of chitchat. I said irritably, "Let's quit wasting time. Remember what I told you. We have air, water, and power for forty-eight hours, and that's it. Don't count on any margin. The water might last a little longer than the others, but you need the other two things to stay alive. Try not to work too hard. The less you metabolize, the less your waste-disposal system has to handle. If we find a tunnel and get in, maybe we can eat some of those emergency rations over there—provided the tunnel's unbreached and hasn't heated up too much in the last couple hundred thousand years. Otherwise, don't even think about food. As to sleeping, forget it; maybe while the drills are going we can catch a couple of naps, but—"

"Now who's wasting time? You've told me all this stuff before." But her voice was still cheery.

So we climbed into the igloo and started work.

The first thing we had to do was to clear out some of the tailings that had already begun to accumulate where we'd left the drill going. The usual way, of course, is to reverse and redirect the augers. We couldn't waste drilling time that way; it would have meant taking them away from cutting the shaft. We had to do it the hard way, namely manually.

It was hard, all right. Heatsuits are uncomfortable to begin with. When you have to work in them, they're miserable. When the work is both hard physically and complicated by the cramped space inside an igloo that already contains two people and a working drill, it's next to impossible.

We did it anyway.

Cochenour hadn't lied to me about Dorrie. She was as good a partner as any man I'd ever had. The big question before us was whether that was going to be good enough. Because there was another question, which was bothering me more and more every minute, and that was whether I was still as good as a man.

Lord knew, I wasn't feeling good. The headache was really pounding at me, and when I moved suddenly I found myself close to blacking out. It all seemed suspiciously like the prognosis they'd given me at the Quackery. To be sure, they'd promised me three weeks before acute hepatic failure, but that hadn't been meant to include this sort of bone-breaking work. I had to figure that I was on plus time already.

That was a disconcerting way to figure.

Especially when the first ten hours went by ... and I realized that our shaft was down lower than the soundings had shown the tunnel to be ... and no luminous blue tailings had come in sight.

We were drilling a dry hole.

Now, if we had had plenty of time and the airbody close by, this would have been no more than an annoyance. Maybe a really big annoyance, sure, but nothing like a disaster. All it would have meant was that I'd get back into the airbody, clean up, get a good night's sleep, eat a meal, and recheck the trace. Probably we were just digging in the wrong spot. All right, next step would be to dig in the right one. Study the terrain, pick a spot, ignite another igloo, start up the drills, and try, try again.

That's what we *would* have done.

But we didn't have any of those advantages. We didn't have the airbody. We had no chance for food or a decent sleep. We were out of igloos. We didn't have the trace to look at—and time was running out on us, and I was feeling lousier every minute.

I crawled out of the igloo, sat down in the next thing there was

to the lee of the wind, and stared up at the scudding yellow-green sky.

There ought to be something to do, if I could only think what it was.

I ordered myself to think.

Let's see, I said to myself. Could I maybe uproot the igloo and move it to another spot?

No. That was a no-go. I could break the igloo loose with the augers, but the minute it was free the winds would catch it and it would be good-bye, Charlie. I'd never see that igloo again. Plus there would be no way to make it gastight anyway.

Well, then, how about drilling without an igloo?

Possible, I judged. Pointless, though. Suppose we did hit lucky and hole in? Without a sealed igloo to lock out those ninety thousand millibars of hot, destructive air, we'd destroy anything fragile inside before we got a look at it.

I felt a nudge on my shoulder and discovered that Dorrie was sitting next to me. She didn't ask any questions, didn't try to say anything at all. I guess it was all clear enough without talking about it.

By my suit chronometer thirteen hours were gone. That left thirty-some before Cochenour would come back to get us. I didn't see any point in spending it all sitting there.

But, on the other hand, I didn't see any point in doing anything else.

Of course, I thought, I could always go to sleep for a while . . . and then I woke up, and realized that that was what I had been doing.

Dorrie was curled up beside me, also asleep.

You may wonder how a person can sleep in the teeth of a south polar thermal gale. It isn't all that hard. All it takes is that you be wholly worn out, and wholly despairing. Sleeping isn't just to knit that old raveled sleave, it is a good way to shut the world off when the world is too lousy to face. As ours was.

But Venus may be the last refuge of the Puritan ethic. On Venus you *work*. The ones who don't feel that way get selected out early, because they don't survive.

It was crazy, of course. In any logical estimate I knew I was as good as dead, but I felt I had to be doing something. I eased away from Dorrie, making sure her suit was belted to the hold-tight ring at the base of the igloo, and stood up.

It took a great deal of concentration for me to be able to stand up. That was all right. It was almost as good as sleeping at keeping thoughts of the world out.

It occurred to me—I admit that even then it seemed like no more than an outside possibility—that something good had happened while Dorrie and I were asleep. Something like—oh, let's say . . . oh, maybe that there still might be eight or ten live Heechee in the tunnel . . . and maybe they'd heard us knocking and opened up the bottom of the shaft for us. So I crawled into the igloo to see if they had.

Nope. They hadn't. I peered down the shaft to make sure, but it was still just a blind hole that disappeared into dirty dark at the end of the light from my head lamp. I swore at the inhospitable Heechee—for being nonexistent, I guess—and kicked some tailings down the hole onto their absent heads.

The Puritan ethic was itching at me somewhere. I wondered

what I ought to be doing. I couldn't think of too many choices. Die? Well, sure, but I was well on my way to doing that as fast as I could. Wasn't there something constructive?

The Puritan ethic reminded me that you always ought to leave a place the way you found it, so I hauled the drills up on the eight-to-one winch and left them hanging neatly while I kicked some more tailings down the useless hole. When I had made enough space for a place to sit, I sat down and thought things over.

I mused about what we had done wrong—not with a view toward doing it right, you see, but more like an old chess puzzle. How had we missed finding a tunnel?

After some time of cloudy cogitation, I thought I knew the answer to that.

It had to do with what an autosonic trace was like. People like Dorrie and Cochenour have the idea that a seismic trace is like one of those underground maps of downtown Dallas that shows all the sewers and utility conduits and water pipes and subways, marked so if you need to get into one of them you can just dig down where it says and you'll find what you want right there.

It isn't exactly like that. The trace is more probabilistic. It comes out as a sort of hazy approximation. It is built up, minute by minute, by the echoes from the pinger. It looks like a band of spiderweb shadows, much wider than any actual tunnel would be and very fuzzy at the edges. When you look at the trace, you know that the best it's telling you is that there's something that makes the shadows. Maybe it's a rock interface or a pocket of gravel. Hopefully it's a Heechee dig. Whatever it is, it's there somewhere, but you don't know just where, exactly. If a tunnel is ten meters wide, which is fair average for a Heechee connecting link, the shadow trace is sure to look like fifty, and may appear to be a hundred.

So where do you dig?

That's where the art of prospecting comes in. You have to make an informed guess.

Maybe you dig in the exact geometrical center—as it is given you to see where the center is. That's the easiest way. Or maybe you dig where the shadows are densest, which is the way the most experienced prospectors do. That works as well as anything else.

But that's not good enough for smart, skilled old Audee Walthers. I do it my own way. What I do, I try to think like a Heechee. I look at the trace as a whole and try to see what points the Heechee might have been trying to connect. Then I plot an imaginary course between them, where I would have put the tunnel if I'd been the Heechee engineer in charge, and I dig where I would have planted the thing in the first place.

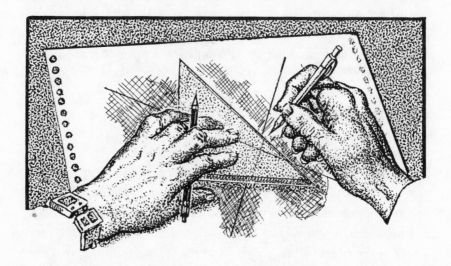

That's what I had done. Evidently I had done it wrong.

Of course, there was one good way I could have gone wrong: the trace could have been a pocket of gravel.

That was a really good possible explanation, but not a useful one. If there had never been a tunnel there in the first place we were just all out of luck. What I wanted was a more hopeful answer, and in a fuzzy-brained sort of way, I began to think I saw one.

I visualized the way the trace had looked on the scope. I had set the airbody down as close to that as I could manage.

Then, of course, I couldn't dig right there, because the airbody was on top of it. So I'd set the igloo up a few meters upslope.

I began to believe that those few meters were what made us miss.

That fuzzy conjecture pleased my fuzzy brain. It explained everything. It was admirable of me, I told myself, to figure it all out in my present state. Of course, I couldn't see that it made any practical difference. If I'd had another igloo I would have been glad to move back to where the airbody had been and try again, assuming I could live long enough to get all that done.

But that didn't mean much, because I didn't have another igloo.

So I sat on the edge of the dark shaft, nodding approvingly to myself over the intelligent way I had thought the problem through, dangling my legs, and now and then sweeping some tailings back in. I think all that was part of some kind of death wish, because I know that I thought, every once in a while, that the nicest thing for me to do just then would be to jump in and pull the tailings down over me.

But the Puritan ethic didn't want me to do that.

Anyway, I would have only solved my own personal problem that way. It wouldn't have done a thing for young Dorotha Keefer, snoring away outside in the thermal gale. I worried about Dorotha Keefer. I wanted something better for her than a life of chancy, sordid scrounging in the Spindle. She was too sweet and kind and—

It struck me as a revelation that one of the reasons for my hostility to Boyce Cochenour had been that he had Dorrie Keefer and I didn't.

That was kind of interesting to think about, too. Suppose, I thought, tasting the bad flavors inside my mouth and feeling my head begin to pound—suppose Cochenour's suit had ruptured when the drill fell on him and he had died right there. Suppose (going a little farther) we'd then found the tunnel, and it was all we wanted from it, and we went back to the Spindle and got rich, and Dorrie and I had—

I spent a lot of time thinking about what Dorrie and I might have done if things had gone just a little different way and all that had happened to be true.

But they hadn't, and it wasn't.

I kicked some more scraps down into the shaft. The tunnel, I was now pretty well convinced, couldn't be more than a few meters away from where that shaft had bottomed out empty. I thought of climbing down into it and scraping away with my gloves.

It seemed like a good idea at the time.

I'm not sure how much of what I was thinking was plain day-dreamy whimsy, and how much the bizarre delusions of a very sick man. I kept thinking strange things. I thought how nice it would be if there were Heechee still in there, and when I climbed down to scratch my way to the tunnel I could just knock on the first blue wall material I came to and they'd open it up and let me in.

That would have been very nice. I even had a picture of what they were going to look like: sort of friendly and godlike. Maybe they would wear togas and offer me scented wines and rare fruits. Maybe they could even speak English, so I could talk to them and ask some of the questions that were on my mind. "Heechee, what did you really use the prayer fans for?" I could ask him. Or, "Listen, Heechee, I hate to be a nuisance, but do you have anything in your medicine chest that will keep me from dying?" Or, "Heechee, I'm sorry we messed up your front yard, and I'll try to clean it up for you."

Maybe it was that last thought that made me push more of the tailings back into the shaft. I didn't have anything better to do. And, who could tell, maybe they'd appreciate it.

After a while I had it more than half full and I'd run out of tailings, except for the ones that were pushed outside the igloo. I didn't have the strength to go after them. I looked for something else to do. I reset the augers, replaced the dull blades with the last sharp ones we had, pointed them in the general direction of a twenty-degree offset angle downslope, and turned them on.

It wasn't until I noticed that Dorrie was standing next to me, helping me steady the augers for the first meter or two of cut, that I realized I had made a plan. I didn't remember it. I didn't even remember when Dorrie had wakened and come into the igloo.

It probably wasn't a bad plan, I thought. Why not try an offset cut? Did we have any better way to spend our time?

We did not. We cut.

When the drills stopped bucking in our hands and settled down to chew through the rock and we could leave them, I cleared a space at the side of the igloo and shoved tailings out for a while.

Then we just sat there, watching the drills spit rock chips out of the new hole. We didn't speak.

Presently I fell asleep again.

I didn't wake up until Dorrie pounded on my helmet. We were buried in tailings. They glowed blue, so bright they almost hurt my eyes.

The augers must have been scratching at the Heechee wall material for an hour or more. They had actually worn pits into it.

When we looked down, we could see the round, bright, blue eye of the tunnel staring up at us. She was a beauty, all right.

We didn't speak.

Somehow I managed to kick and wriggle my way through the drift to the crawl-through. I got the lock closed and sealed, after kicking a couple of cubic meters of rock outside.

Then I began fumbling through the pile of refuse for the flame drills.

Ultimately I found them. Somehow. Ultimately I managed to get them shipped and primed.

We ducked back out of range as I fired them. I watched the

bright spot of light that bounced out of the shaft make a pattern on the roof of the igloo.

Then there was a sudden, short scream of gas, and a clatter as the loose fragments at the bottom of the shaft dropped free.

We had cut into the Heechee tunnel.

It was unbreached and waiting for us. Our beauty was a virgin. We took her maidenhead with all love and reverence and entered into her.

XII

I must have blacked out again, because when I realized where I was I was on the floor of the tunnel. My helmet was open. So were the side-zips of my heatsuit. I was breathing stale, foul air that had to be a quarter of a million years old and smelled every minute of it.

But it was air.

It was denser than Earth-normal and a lot less humid, but the partial pressure of oxygen was close enough to the same. I was proving that by the fact that I had been breathing it without dying.

Next to me on the floor was Dorrie Keefer.

Her helmet was open, too. The blue Heechee wall light didn't flatter her complexion, so she looked about as ghastly as a pretty girl can. At first I wasn't sure she was breathing. But in spite of the way she looked, her pulse was going, her lungs were functioning, and when she felt me poking at her she opened her eyes.

"God, I'm beat," she said. "But we made it!"

I didn't say anything. She'd said it all for both of us. We sat there, grinning foolishly at each other, looking like Halloween masks in the blue Heechee glow.

That was about all I was able to do just then. I was feeling very light-headed. I had my hands full just comprehending the fact that I was alive. I didn't want to endanger that odds-against precarious fact by moving around.

I wasn't comfortable, though, and after a moment I realized that I was very hot. I closed up my helmet to shut out some of the heat, but the smell inside was so bad that I opened it again, figuring that the heat was better.

It then occurred to me to wonder why the heat was only unpleasant, instead of instantly, incineratingly fatal.

Energy transport through a Heechee wall-material surface is slow, but not hundreds of thousands of years slow. My sad, sick old brain ruminated that thought around for a while and finally staggered to a conclusion: At least until quite recently, maybe some centuries or thousands of years at most, this tunnel had been kept artificially cool. So, I told myself sagely, there had to be some sort of automatic machinery. Wow, I said to myself. That ought to be worth finding all by itself. Broken down or not, it could be the kind of thing fortunes are built on . . .

And that made me remember why we had come there in the first place. I looked up the corridor and down, hungry for the first site of the Heechee loot that might make us all well again.

When I was a schoolkid in Amarillo Central, my favorite teacher was a crippled lady named Miss Stevenson. She used to tell us stories out of Bulfinch and Homer.

Miss Stevenson spoiled one whole weekend for me with the sad story of one Greek fellow whose biggest ambition was to become a god. I gathered that was a fairly ordinary goal for a bright young Greek in those days, though I'm not sure how often they made it. This man started out with a few big steps up the ladder—he was already a king, of a little place in Lydia—but he wanted more. He wanted divinity. The gods even let him come to Olympus, and it looked as though he had it made . . . until he fouled up.

I don't remember the details of what he did wrong, except that it had something to do with a dog and some nasty trick he played on one of the gods by getting him to eat his own son. (Those Greeks had pretty primitive ideas of humor, I guess.) Whatever it was, they punished him for it. What he got was solitary confinement—for eternity—and he served it standing neck deep in a cool lake in hell but unable to drink. Every time he opened his lips the water pulled away. The fellow's name was Tantalus ... and in that Heechee tunnel I thought I had a lot in common with him.

We found the treasure trove we were looking for, all right. But we couldn't reach it.

It seemed that what we had dug into wasn't the main tunnel after all. It was a sort of right-angled, Thielly-tube detour in the tunnel, and it was blocked at both ends.

"What do you suppose it is?" Dorrie asked wistfully, trying to peer through the gaps in the ten-ton slabs of Heechee metal before us. "Do you suppose it could be that weapon you were talking about?"

I blinked my fuzzy eyes. There were machines of all kinds there, and irregular mounds of things that might have been containers for

other things, and some objects that seemed to have rotted and spilled their contents, also rotted, on the floor. But we hadn't the strength to get at them.

I stood there with my helmet pressed against the side of one of the slabs, feeling like Alice peering into her tiny garden without the bottle of drink-me. "All I know for sure," I said, "is that, whatever it is, there's more of it there than anybody ever found before."

And I slumped to the floor, exhausted and sick and, all the same, feeling very contented with the world.

Dorrie sat down next to me, in front of that barred gate to Eden, and we rested for a moment.

"Gram would've been pleased," she murmured.

"Oh, sure," I agreed, feeling a little drunk. "Gram?"

"My grandmother," she explained, and then maybe I blacked out again. When I heard what she was saying again, she was talking about how her grandmother had refused to marry Cochenour, long and long ago. It seemed to matter to Dorotha Keefer, so I tried politely to pay attention, but some of it didn't make a lot of sense.

"Wait a minute," I said. "She didn't want him because he was *poor*?"

"No, no! Not because he was poor, although he was that. Because he was going off to the oil fields, and she wanted somebody steadier. Like my grandfather. And then when Boyce came by a year ago—"

"He gave you a job," I said, nodding to show I was following, "as his girlfriend."

"No, damn it!" she said, annoyed with me. "In his office. The—other part came later. We fell in love."

"Oh, right," I said. I wasn't looking for an argument.

She said stiffly, "He's really a sweet man, Audee. Outside of business, I mean. And he would've done anything for me."

"He could've married you," I pointed out, just to keep the conversation going.

"No, Audee," she said seriously, "he couldn't. He wanted to get married. I was the one who said no."

She turned down all that money? I blinked at her. I didn't have to ask the question; she knew what it was.

"When I marry," she said, "I want kids, and Boyce wouldn't hear of it. He said if I'd caught him when he was a lot younger, maybe seventy-five or eighty, he might've taken a chance, but now he was just too old to be raising a family."

"Then you ought to be looking around for a replacement, shouldn't you?"

She looked at me in that blue glow. "He needs me," she said simply. "Now more than ever."

I mulled that over for a while. Then it occurred to me to check the time.

It was nearly forty-six hours since he had left us. He was due back any time.

And if he came back while we were doddering around in here—I realized, foggily, bit by bit—then ninety thousand millibars of poison gas would hammer in on us. It would kill us if we had our

suits open. Besides that, it would damage our virgin tunnel. The corrosive scouring of that implosion of gas might easily wreck all those lovely things behind the barrier.

"We have to go back," I told Dorrie, showing her the time. She smiled.

"Temporarily," she said, and we got up, took a last look at those treasures of Tantalus behind the bars, and started back to our shaft to the igloo.

After the cheerful blue glow of the Heechee tunnel, the igloo was more cramped and miserable than ever before.

What was worse was that my cloudy brain nagged me into remembering that we shouldn't even stay inside it. Cochenour might remember to lock in and out of both ends of the crawl-through when he got there—any minute now—but he also might not. I couldn't take the chance on letting the hot hammer of air in on our pretties.

I tried to think of a way of plugging the shaft, maybe by pushing all the tailings back in again, but although my brain wasn't working very well I could see that that was stupid.

So the only way to solve that problem was for us to wait outside in the breezy Venusian weather. The one consolation was that it wouldn't be too much longer to wait. The other part of that was that we weren't equipped for a very long wait. The little watch dial next to our life-support meters, all running well into the warning red now, showed that Cochenour should in fact have arrived by now.

He wasn't there, though.

I squeezed into the crawl-through with Dorrie, locked us both through, and we waited.

I felt a scratching on my helmet and discovered Dorrie was plugging into my jack. "Audee, I'm really very tired," she told me. It didn't sound like a complaint, only a factual report of something she thought I probably should know about.

"You might as well go to sleep," I told her. "I'll keep watch. Cochenour will be here pretty soon, and I'll wake you up."

I suppose she took my advice, because she lowered herself down, pausing to let me take her talk line out of my helmet jack. Then she stretched out next to the tie-down clips and left me to think in peace.

I wasn't grateful. I wasn't enjoying what I was beginning to think.

Still Cochenour didn't come.

I tried to think through the significance of that. Of course, there could have been lots of reasons for a delay. He could've gotten lost. He could have been challenged by the military. He could have crashed the airbody.

But there was a much nastier possibility, and it seemed to make more sense than all of them.

The time dial told me he was nearly five hours late, and the life-support meters told me that we were right up against the "empty" line for power, near it for air, and well past it for water. If we hadn't had the remaining tunnel gases to breathe for a few hours, saving the air in our tanks, we would have been dead by now.

Cochenour couldn't have known that we would find breathable air in the Heechee tunnel. He must believe that we were dead.

The man hadn't lied about himself. He had told me he was a bad loser.

So he had decided not to lose.

In spite of my fuzzy brain, I could understand what had gone on in his. When push came to shove the bastard in him won out. He had worked out an endgame maneuver that would pull a win out of all his defeats.

I could visualize him, as clearly as though I were in the airbody with him. Watching his clocks as our lives ticked away. Cooking himself an elegant little lunch. Playing the rest of the Tchaikovsky ballet music, maybe, while he waited for us to get through dying.

It wasn't a really frightening thought to me. I was close enough to being dead anyway for the difference to be pretty much of a technicality . . . and tired enough of being trapped in that foul heatsuit to accept almost any deliverance, even the final one.

But I wasn't the only person affected here.

The girl was also involved. The one tiny little rational thought that stayed in my half-poisoned brain was that it was just unfair for Cochenour to let us both die. Me, yes, all right; I could see that from his point of view I was easily expendable. Her, no.

I realized I ought to do something, and after considering what that might be for a while I beat on her suit until she moved a little. After some talk through the phone jacks I managed to make her understand she had to go back down into the tunnel, where at least she could breathe.

Then I got ready for Cochenour's return.

There were two things he didn't know. He didn't know we'd found any breathable air, and he didn't know we could tap the drill batteries for additional power.

In all the freaked-out fury of my head, I was still capable of that much consecutive thought. I could surprise him—if he didn't stay away too much longer, anyway. I could stay alive for a few hours yet . . .

And then, when he came to find us dead and see what prize we had won for him, he would find me waiting.

And so he did.

It must have been a terrible shock to him when he entered the crawl-through to the igloo with the monkey wrench in his hand, leaned over me, and found I was still alive and able to move, when he had expected only a well-done roast of meat.

If I had had any doubt about his intentions it was resolved when he swung immediately at my helmet. Age, busted leg, and surprise didn't slow his reflexes a bit. But he had to change position to get a good swing in the cramped space inside the crawl-through, and, being not only alive but pretty nearly conscious, I managed to roll away in time. And I already had the drill ready to go in my arms.

The drill caught him right in the chest.

I couldn't see his face, but I can guess at his expression.

After that, it was only a matter of doing five or six impossible things at once. Things like getting Dorrie up out of the tunnel and into the airbody. Like getting myself in after her, and sealing up and setting a course. All those impossible things . . . and one more, that was harder than any of them, but very important to me. Dorrie didn't know why I insisted on bringing Cochenour's body back. I think she thought it was a kind gesture of reverence to the dead on my part, but I didn't straighten her out just then.

I just about totaled the airbody when we landed, but we were suited up and strapped in, and when the ground crews came out from the Spindle to investigate Dorrie and I were still alive.

XIII

They had to patch me and rehydrate me for three days before they could even think about putting my new liver in. It was a wonder it had survived its ordeal, but they'd whipped it out and put it on nutrient pumps as soon as they got their hands on it. By the time it was ready to be transplanted into me it had had its allergenic nature tamed and was as good as any liver ever was—good enough, anyway, to keep me alive.

They kept me sedated most of the time. The quacks woke me up every couple of hours to give me another bout of feedback training on how to monitor my hepatic flows—they said there was no point giving me a new liver if I didn't know how to use it—and other people kept waking me up to ask me questions, but it was all dreamlike. I didn't much want to be awake just then. Being awake was all sickness and pain and nagging, and I could have wished for the old days back again—when they just would have knocked me out with anesthesia until they were through—except, of course, that in the old days I would have died.

But by the fourth day I hardly hurt at all—well, except when I moved. And they were letting me take my fluids by mouth instead of the other way.

I realized I was going to be alive for a while. That was very good news, and, once I believed it, I began to take more interest in what was going on.

The Quackery was in its spring mood, which I appreciated. Of course, there's no such thing as a season in the Spindle, but the quacks get all sentimental about tradition and ties with the Mother Planet, so they create seasons for themselves. The current one was made by scenes of fleecy white clouds playing across the wall panels, and the air from the ventilator ducts smelled of lilac and green leaves.

"Happy spring," I said to Dr. Morius while he was examining me.

"Shut up," he said to me. He shifted a couple of the needles that pincushioned my abdomen, watching the readings on the telltales. "Um," he muttered.

"I'm glad you think so," I said.

He disregarded my remark. Dr. Morius doesn't like humorous

conversation unless it comes from him. He pursed his lips and pulled out a couple of the needles. "Well, let's see, Walthers. We've taken out the splenoveal shunt. Your new liver is functioning well—no sign of rejection—but you're not flushing wastes through as fast as you ought to. You'll have to work on that. We've got your ion levels back up to something like a human being, and most of your tissues have a little moisture in them again. Altogether," he said, scratching his head in thought, "yes, in general, I would say you're alive. So I think probably the operation was a success."

"That's very witty," I said.

"You've got some people waiting for you," he went on. "Vastra's Third and your lady friend. They brought you some clothes."

That interested me. "Does that mean I'm getting out?" I asked.

"Like right now," he told me. "They'll have to keep you in bed awhile, but your rent's run out. We need the space for paying customers."

Now, one of the advantages of having clean blood in my brains instead of the poisonous soup it had been living on was that I could begin to think reasonably clearly.

So I knew right away that good old comical Dr. Morius was making another of his little jokes. "Paying customers." I wouldn't have been there if I hadn't been a paying patient. Though I couldn't imagine what my bills were being paid with, I was willing to keep my curiosity in check until I was outside the Quackery.

That didn't take long. The quacks packed me in wetsheets, and Dorrie and the Third of Vastra's House rolled me through the Spindle to Sub Vastra's place. Dorrie was pale and tired still—the last couple of weeks hadn't been much of a vacation for either of us—but needing nothing more than a little rest, she said. Sub's First had kicked some of the kids out of a cubicle and cleared it out for us, and his Third fussed over both of us, feeding us up on lamb broth and that flat hard bread they like, before tucking us in for a good long rest. There was only the one bed, but Dorrie didn't seem to mind. Anyway, at that point the question was academic. Later on, not so academic. After a couple of days of that I was on my feet and as good as I ever was.

By then I found out who had paid my bill at the Quackery.

For about a minute I had hoped it was me—quickly filthy rich from the priceless spoils of our tunnel—but I knew that was an illusion. The tunnel had been right on the military reservation. Nobody was ever going to own anything in it but the military.

If we'd been hale and hearty we could have gotten around that, with a little inventive lying. We could have carted some of the things off to another tunnel and declared them, and almost certainly we would have gotten away with it . . . but not the way we were. We'd been a lot too near dead to conceal anything.

So the military had taken it all.

Still, they'd showed something I never had suspected. They did have a kind of a heart. Atrophied and flinty, yes, but a heart. They'd gone into the dig while I was still getting glucose enemas in my sleep, and they'd been pleased with what they'd found. They decided to pay me a kind of finder's fee. Not much, to be sure. But enough to save my life. Enough to meet the Quackery's bill for all their carpentry on me, and even enough left over to put some in the bank and pay the back rent on my own place, so Dorrie and I could move in when Vastra's House decided we were well enough to be on our own.

Of course, they hadn't had to pay for the transplant liver itself. That hadn't cost anything at all.

For a while it bothered me that the military wouldn't say what they'd found. I did my best to find out. I even tried to get Sergeant Littleknees drunk so I could worm it out of her, when she came to the Spindle on furlough. That didn't work. Dorrie was right there, and how drunk can you get one girl when another girl is right there watching you? Probably Amanda Littleknees didn't know, anyhow. Probably nobody did except a few specialists.

But it had to be something big, because of the cash award, and most of all because they didn't prosecute us for trespassing on the military reservation. And so we get along all right, the two of us. Or the three of us.

Dorrie turned out to be really good at selling imitation prayer fans and fire-pearls to the Terry tourists, especially when her pregnancy began to show. We were both kind of celebrities, of course. She kept us in eating money until the high season started, and by then I had found out that my status as a famous tunnel discoverer was worth something, so I parlayed it into a cash loan and a new airbody. We're doing pretty well, for tunnel-rats. I've promised I'll marry her if our kid turns out to be a boy, but as a matter of fact I'm going to do it anyway. She was a great help at the dig.

Especially with my own private project.

Dorrie couldn't have known just what I wanted to bring Cochenour's body back for. She didn't argue, though. Sick and wretched as she was, she helped me get the cadaver into the airbody lock for the return to the Spindle.

Actually, I wanted that body very much—one piece of it, anyway.

It's not really a *new* liver, of course. Probably it's not even secondhand. Heaven knows where Cochenour bought it, but I'm sure it wasn't his original equipment.

But it works.

And, bastard though he was, I kind of liked him in a way, and I don't mind at all the fact that I've got a part of him with me always.

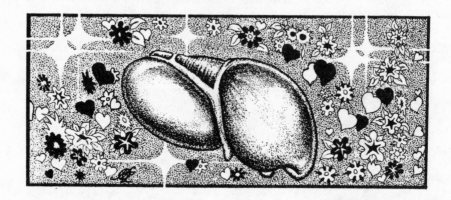

PART THREE

THE GATEWAY ASTEROID

The greatest treasure the Heechee tunnels on Venus had to offer had already been discovered, though the first discoverers didn't know it. No one else knew, either—at least, no one except a solitary tunnel-rat named Sylvester Macklin, and he was not in a position to tell anybody what he had found.

Sylvester Macklin had discovered a Heechee spaceship.

If Macklin had reported his find he would have become the richest man in the solar system. He also would have lived to enjoy his wealth. But Sylvester Macklin was as crotchety a loner as any other tunnel-rat, and he did something quite different.

He saw that the ship looked to be in good condition. Maybe, he thought, he could even fly it.

Unfortunately for himself, he succeeded.

Macklin's ship did exactly what any Heechee ship was designed to do, and the Heechee were marvelously great designers. No one knows exactly what processes of thought and experiment and deduction Macklin went through when he blundered onto the wonderful find. He didn't survive to tell anyone. Still, obviously at some point he must have gotten into the ship and closed its hatch and begun poking and prodding at the things that looked as though they ought to be its controls.

As people later well learned, on the board of every Heechee ship is a thing shaped like a cow's teat. It is the thing that makes the ship go. When it is squeezed it is like slipping an automatic-shift car into "drive." The ship moves out. Where it goes to depends on what course was set into its automatic navigation systems.

Macklin didn't do anything about setting any particular course, naturally. He didn't know how.

So the ship did what its Heechee designers had programmed it to do in such an event. It simply returned to the place it had come from when its Heechee pilot had left it, half a million years ago.

As it happened, that place was an asteroid.

It was an odd asteroid in several respects. Astronomically it was odd, because its orbit was at right angles to the ecliptic. For that reason, although it was a fair-sized chunk of rock and not far from Earth's own orbit at times, it had never been discovered by human astronomers.

The other odd thing about it was that it had been converted into a sort of parking garage for Heechee spacecraft. In total, there were nearly a thousand of the ships there.

What there was not any of anywhere on the asteroid was anything to eat or drink. So Sylvester Macklin, who could have been

the richest man in history, wound up as just one more starved-to-death corpse.

But before he died Macklin managed to get off a signal to Earth. It wasn't a call for help. No one could reach him in time to save his life. Macklin knew that. He accepted the fact that he would die; he just wanted people to know in what an unsuspected marvel of a place he was dying. And after a while other astronauts, flying the clumsy human rockets of the time, came to investigate.

What they found was the gateway to the universe.

Within the next decade the Gateway asteroid had become the center of mankind's most profitable industry, the exploration of the galaxy.

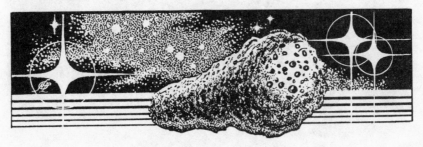

Macklin didn't own the Gateway asteroid, of course, in spite of the fact that he had discovered it. His luck wasn't that good. He didn't own anything, being dead.

Anyway, it soon became obvious that Gateway was much too important to be owned by any individual, or even by any single nation. The United Nations fought over the question for years, in Security Council and General Assembly—and, more than once, almost with guns and aircraft outside the UN itself. What the world powers wound up with was the Gateway Corporation, a five-power consortium that was set up to control it.

The Gateway asteroid was not a very congenial place for people to live—of course, it had never been designed for human people. It had been designed for the Heechee, and they had stripped it bare before they left. It was a chunk of rock the size of Manhattan, laced through and through with tunnels and chambers and not much else. The thing wasn't even round. One Gateway prospector described it as shaped "more or less like a badly planned pear that the birds had been pecking at." Its internal structure resembled the layers of an onion. The outer shell was where the Heechee ships were docked, their lander ports snuggled into hatch chambers. (Those chambers were the things that looked from the outside like bird peckings.)

Then, inside, there were layers with great open spaces which the humans used for storing supplies and parts, and for the large water reservoir they called "Lake Superior." Closer to the center were the residential tunnels, lined with small rooms like monastery cells, where the humans lived while they waited for their ships. In the heart of the asteroid was a spindle-shaped cavern. The Heechee seemed to like spindle-shaped spaces, though no one knew why. Gateway's tenants used this one for a meeting place—and drinking place, and gambling place, and a place to try to forget what lay ahead of them.

Gateway didn't smell good. Air was precious. It didn't *feel* good, either, at least not to fresh prospectors just up from Earth. The asteroid had a slow spin, so there was a sort of microgravity, but there wasn't much of it. Anyone who made a sudden move anywhere in Gateway was likely to find himself floating away.

Of course, no one ever looked at the Gateway asteroid as a resort paradise. There was only one reason why any human being would be willing to put up with its expense, its inaccessibility, its discomforts, and its stink, and the reason was the Heechee spaceships.

Flying a Heechee spaceship took a lot of courage, and not much else. Each ship was like every other ship in its class. The biggest of them, the Fives, were not very big—about the same volume of space as a hotel bathroom, and that to be shared by five people. The ships called the Ones (because they could hold only one person for any length of time) were not much bigger than the bathtub itself. Each ship contained a minimum of fittings, and most of the fittings were of unknown importance. There was always a golden coil that seemed to have something to do with the ship's drive, because it was observed to change color at start, finish, and turnaround of each trip. There was always a diamond-shaped golden box about the size of a coffin, too. In a few of the ships there was an even more mysterious

134

device that looked like a twisted rod of crystal in a black ebon base; it didn't seem to do anything at all (but, as it turned out much later, was capable of some truly astonishing feats). No one knew exactly what was inside any of those things, because whenever anyone tried

to open one it exploded. And then there was the control system, with a curious, painful forked bench to sit on before it. Knurled knobs, flashing lights, the go-teat—they were what made the ship go.

Of course, the ships lacked a great many things that human

beings really didn't want to get along without: the people who ultimately flew them had some human furnishings added, like freez-
ers, more comfortable seats, bunks, cooking tools—and a whole
catalogue of cameras, radio antennae, and scientific instruments of
all kinds.

There was nothing hard about flying a Heechee ship. Anybody
could learn as much as anybody else knew in half an hour: you
fiddled around with the course-setting wheels, pretty much at random because no one knew what the settings meant. Actually (it was
learned, much later and at great cost) there were some 14,922 separate destinations preprogrammed into the 731 operable ships on the
asteroid—there were about another 200 ships that simply didn't
work at all. But it took a lot of time, and a lot of lives, to find out
what some of those destinations were.

Then, when you had set up some combination (and crossed
your fingers, or yourself), you squeezed the go-teat. After that you
were on your way. That was all there was to it.

For that reason, anybody could become a prospector. Anybody,
that is, who was willing to pay his way to Gateway and then to pay
the steep charges for air, food, water, and living space while he was
in the asteroid . . . and who was brave enough, or desperate enough,
to take his chances on a highly likely and often very nasty death.

Over the years a great many human beings escaped from their Earthside poverty to take their chances in a Gateway ship. First and last, there were 13,842 of these gold-rush gamblers, in those chancy years before exact navigation of a Heechee ship became possible and the random exploration program was discontinued.

Quite a few of the prospectors survived. Many became famous. A few became vastly rich. And no one remembers the others.

PART FOUR

THE STARSEEKERS

When one of those bold, faintly crazy early prospectors set out in a Heechee spacecraft, he didn't expect the ship to go exactly where he wanted it to go. He (or, almost as often, she) could never count on that for many reasons, not least because none of those early prospectors had any idea what destinations were worth aiming for. But that ignorance carried no penalty, anyway. Since no Gateway prospector knew how to navigate a Heechee ship, the first ships followed whatever destination settings had been left on the board by the last long-ago Heechee pilot.

Considering the risks, it was a good thing for those early Gateway prospectors that the Heechee had been so much like human beings in important ways. For instance, the Heechee had possessed the primate-human itch of curiosity—in fact, they had a lot of it. That meant that a lot of the preprogrammed destinations were to places that human beings also found interesting to look at. They were just as interesting to human beings as they had been to the old Heechee, and the particular branch of the human race that delighted most in what the first waves of Gateway explorers found was the astronomers. Those astronomical people had become very ingenious at teasing information from whatever photons landed in their instruments—whether those photons were visible light, X-rays, infrared, whatever. But photons couldn't tell them everything they wanted to know. The human astronomers sighed over their knowledge that there was such a *lot* of stuff out there that didn't radiate at all—black holes, planets, heaven knew what! They could only guess at such things.

Now, with the Heechee spacecraft, someone could go out and see them firsthand!

That was a pretty wonderful break for astronomers . . . although often enough it turned out to be a lot less wonderful for the men and women who went out to look.

The trouble with astronomy, from the point of view of the prospector who had just risked his life on a shot-in-the-dark voyage on a Heechee ship, was that you couldn't sell a neutron star. What the prospectors were after was *money*. That meant that, if they were lucky, they might find some kind of high-tech Heechee gadgets that could be brought back and studied and copied and made into fortunes. There wasn't any commercial market for a supernova shell or an interstellar gas cloud; those things just didn't pay the bills.

To deal with that problem, the Gateway Corporation started a program of paying science bonuses to the explorers who came back with great pictures and instrument readings but nothing commercial to sell.

That was virtuous of the Gateway Corporation, to pay off for pure, noncommercial knowledge. It was also a good way of coaxing more hungry humans into those scary and often deadly little ships.

By the time the Gateway Corporation had been in operation for two full years more than one hundred trips had set out, and sixty-two of them had returned, more or less safely. (Not counting the odd prospector who arrived dead, dying, or scared out of his wits.)

The ships had visited at least forty different stars—all kinds of stars: baby blue-white giants, immense and short-lived, like Regulus and Spica and Altair; yellow normal-sequence stars like Procyon A and their dwarf counterparts, like Procyon B; staid G-type stars like the Sun, and their giant yellow relatives, like Capella. The red giants, of the types of Aldebran and Arcturus, and their supergiant counterparts, like Betelgeuse and Antares . . . and their tiny red-dwarf relatives, like Proxima Centauri and Wolf 359.

The astronomers were thrilled. Every trip's harvest triumphantly supported much of what they thought they had known about the birth and death of stars—and demanded quick revisions of much else that they thought they had known, but hadn't. The masters of the Corporation were less delighted. It was all very well to expand the horizons of astronomical science, but the pictures of the twentieth white dwarf looked pretty much like the pictures of

the first. The hungry billions of Earth could not be fed on astronomical photographs. They already had a number of astronomical observatories in orbit. They weren't pleased to see their once-in-a-lifetime treasure trove turned into just one more of them.

But even the Corporation had to be pleased at some of the things the prospectors brought back.

MISSION *PULSAR*

The first big science bonus was paid to a man named Chou Yengbo, and he might not have earned it if he hadn't happened to have taken a few elementary science courses before he discovered that even a college degree couldn't get you a decent job, those days, in Shensi Province.

When Chou's ship came out of the faster-than-light drive, Chou had no trouble figuring out which objects the Heechee had set the controls for.

Actually there were three objects in view. They were weird. The first was wholly unlike anything Chou had ever seen before, even in the holograms of his astronomy course. It wasn't quite like anything any other human being had ever seen before, either, except in imagination. The object was an irregular, cone-shaped splash of light, and even on the viewscreen its colors hurt his eyes.

What the thing looked like was a searchlight beam fanning out through patches of mist. When Chou looked more carefully, magnifying the image, he saw that there was another beam like it, sketchier and fainter and fanning out in the opposite direction. And between the two points of the cones formed by those beams, the third object was something almost too tiny to see.

When he put the magnification up to max, he saw that that something was a puny-looking, unhealthily colored little star.

It was much too small to be a normal star. That limited the possibilities; even so, it took Chou some time to realize that he was in the presence of a pulsar.

Then those Astronomy 101 lessons came back to him. It was Subrahmanyan Chandrasekhar, back in the middle of the twentieth century, who had calculated the genesis of neutron stars. His model was simple. A large star, Chandrasekhar said, uses up its hydrogen fuel and then collapses. It throws off most of the outer sections of itself as a supernova. What is left falls in toward the star's center, at almost the speed of light, compressing most of the star's mass into a volume smaller than a planet—smaller, in fact, than some mountains. This particular sort of collapse can only happen to big stars, Chandrasekhar calculated. They had to be 1.4 times as massive as Earth's Sun, at least, and so that number was called Chandrasekhar's Limit.

After that supernova explosion and collapse has happened, the object that remains—star heavy, asteroid sized—is a "neutron star." It has been crushed together so violently by its own immense gravitation that the electrons of its atoms are driven into its protons, creating the chargeless particles called neutrons. Its substance is so dense that a cubic inch of it weighs two million tons or so; it is like compressing the hugest of Earth's old supertankers into something the size of a coin. Things do not leave a neutron star easily; with that immense, concentrated mass pulling things down to its surface, escape velocity becomes something like 120,000 miles a second. More than that: its rotational energy has been "compressed," too. The blue-white giant star that used to turn on its axis once a week is now a superheavy asteroid-sized thing that whirls around many times a second.

Chou knew there were observations that he had to make—magnetic, X-ray, infrared, and many others. The magnetometer readings were the most important. Neutron stars have superfluid cores and so, as they rotate, they generate intense magnetic fields—just like the Earth. Not really just like the Earth, though, because the neutron star's magnetic field, too, is compressed. It is one trillion times stronger than the Earth's. And as it spins it generates radiation. The radiation can't simply flow out from all parts of the star at once—the lines of magnetic force confine it. It can only escape at the neutron star's north and south magnetic poles.

The magnetic poles of any object aren't necessarily in the same place as its poles of rotation. (The Earth's north magnetic pole is hundreds of miles away from the point where the meridians of longitude meet.) So all the neutron star's radiated energy pours out in a beam, around and around, pointing a little, or sometimes a lot, away from its true rotational poles.

So that was the explanation of the thing Chou was seeing. The cones were the two polar beams from the star that lay between them, north and south, fanning out from its poles. Of course, Chou couldn't see the beams themselves. What he saw were the places

where they illuminated tenuous clouds of gas and dust as they spread out.

The important thing to Chou was that no Earthly astronomer had ever seen them that way. The only way anyone on Earth ever could see the beam from a neutron star was by the chance of being somewhere along the rim of the conical shape the beams described as they rotated. And then what they saw was a high-speed flicker, so fast and regular that the first observer to spot one thought it was the signal from an alien intelligence. They called the signal an "LGM" (for Little Green Men) until they figured out what was causing that sort of stellar behavior.

Then they called the things "pulsars."

Chou got a four-hundred-thousand-dollar science bonus for what he had discovered. He wasn't greedy. He took it and returned to Earth, where he found a new career lecturing to women's clubs and college audiences on what it was like to be a Heechee prospector. He was a great success, because he was one of the first of the breed to return to Earth alive.

Later returnees were less fortunate. For instance, there was—

MISSION *HALO*

In some ways Mission *Halo* was the saddest and most beautiful of all. The mission had been written off as lost, but that turned out to be wrong. The ship wasn't lost. Only its crew was.

The ship was an unarmored Three. When it came back its arrival was a surprise to everyone. The ship had been gone over *three years*. It was a certainty that nobody could have survived so long a trip. In fact, no one had. When the hatch crews on Gateway got the ports open, recoiling from the stench inside, they discovered that Jan Mariekiewicz, Rolph Stret, and Lech Szelikowitz had left a record of their experiences. It was read with compassion by the other prospectors, and with rejoicing by astronomers.

"When we reached two hundred days without turnaround," Stret had written in his diary, "we knew we were out of luck. We drew straws. I won. Maybe I should say I lost, but, anyway, Jan and Lech took their little suicide pills, and I put their bodies in the freezer.

"Turnaround came finally at 271 days. I knew for sure that I wasn't going to make it either, not even with only me alive in the ship. So I've tried rigging everything on automatic. I hope it works. If the ship gets back, please pass on our messages."

As it happened, the messages the crew left never got delivered. There was no one to deliver them to. The messages were all addressed to other Gateway prospectors who had been part of the same shipment up from Central Europe, and that batch wasn't one of the lucky ones. Every one of them had been lost in their own ships.

But the pictures the ship brought back belonged to the whole world.

Stret's jury-rigging had worked. The ship had stopped at its destination. The instruments had thoroughly mapped everything in sight. Then the ship's return had been triggered automatically, while Stret's corpse lay bloating under the controls.

The record showed that their ship had been outside the Milky Way galaxy entirely.

It brought back the first pictures ever seen of our galaxy *from outside*. It showed a couple of fairly nearby stars and one great, distant globular cluster—the stars and clusters of the spherical halo that surrounds our galaxy—but most of all it showed our Milky Way galaxy itself, from core to farthest spiral wisp, with its great, familiar octopus arms: the Perseus arm, the Cygnus arm, the Sagittarius-Carina arm (with our own little Orion arm, the small spur that held the Earth, nearby), as well as the large, distant arm that Earthly astronomers had never seen before. They called it simply "Far Arm" at first, but then it was renamed the Stret-Mariekiewicz-Szelikowitz arm to honor the dead discoverers. And in the center of it all was the great bellying octopus-body mass of core stars, laced with gas and dust clouds, showing the beginnings of the new growing spiral structures that might in another hundred million years become new arms themselves.

They also showed the effects of a structure more interesting still, but not in enough detail to be recognized just then—not until some other events had taught human beings what to look for in the core. All the same, they were beautiful pictures.

Since no one returned from Mission *Halo* alive, there wasn't even a science bonus due, but the Gateway Corporation voted a special exception to the rules. Five million dollars was voted for the heirs of Mariekiewicz, Szelikowitz, and Stret.

It was a generous gesture but, as it turned out, a very inexpensive one. The award went unclaimed. Like so many Gateway prospectors, the three who had manned the ship had no families that anyone could find, and so the Gateway Corporation's bursar quietly, and philosophically, returned the cash to the Corporation's general funds.

The first, best, and brightest hope of any exploration crew was to find a really nice planet with really nice treasures on it. Ultimately some of them did, of course, but it took a while. For a good many orbits after the systematic exploration program began the crews went out and came back with nothing but pictures and hardluck stories—when they came back at all.

But some of the things they had seen were *wonderful*. Volya Shadchuk took a One into the heart of a planetary nebula, greentinged with the radiation from oxygen atoms, and collected fifty thousand dollars. Bill Merrian saw a recurring nova system, red giant's gases being sucked onto a white dwarf; luckily not enough matter had accreted while he was there to blow off in a noval explosion, but he got the fifty thousand and ten percent more for "danger bonus." And then there were the Grantlands.

There were five of the Grantlands—two brothers, their wives, and the eldest son of one of the couples. They reached a globular cluster—ten thousand old stars, mostly red, mostly sliding toward the sunset at the lower right side of the Hertzsprung-Russell diagram as they aged. The cluster was in the galactic halo and, of course, the trip was a long one. None of them survived. The trip took 314 days, and all of them were alive at the time of arrival (but existing on scant rations). They took their pictures. The last of them, the young second wife of one of the brothers, died thirty-three days into the return trip; but the pictures they had taken survived.

The three Schoen sisters were no luckier. They didn't come back at all, either. Again, their ship did, but thoroughly racked and scorched, and of course their bodies inside were barely recognizable.

But they, too, had taken a few pictures before they died. They had been in a reflection nebula—after analysis it was determined that

it was the Great Nebula in Orion, actually visible to the naked eye from Earth. (American Indians called it "the smoking star.") The Schoen sisters must have known they were in trouble as soon as they came out of drive, because they weren't really in space anymore. Oh, it was close to a vacuum—as people on Earth measure a vacuum—but there were as many as three hundred atoms to the cubic centimeter, hundreds of times as many as there should have been in interstellar space.

Still, they looked around, and they started their cameras—just barely. They didn't have much time.

There are four bright young stars in the Orion Nebula, the so-called Trapezium; it is in such nebulae that gas clouds fall together and are born as stars. Astronomers conjectured that the Heechee knew this, and the reason the ship had been set to go there was that Heechee astronomers had been interested in studying the conditions that lead to star formation.

But the Heechee had set that program half a million years before.

A lot had happened in those half million years. There was now a fifth body, an "almost" star, in the Orion Nebula, formed after the Heechee had taken their last look at the area. The new body was called the Becklin-Neugebauer object; it was in its early hydrogen-burning stage, less than a hundred thousand years old. And it seemed that the Schoen sisters had the bad luck to come almost inside it.

MISSION *NAKED BLACK HOLE*

The crew was William Sakyetsu, Marianna Morse, Hal M'Buna, Richard Smith, and Irina Malatesta. All of them had been Out before—Malatesta had done it five times—but luck hadn't favored any of their ventures. None of them had yet made a big enough score to pay their Gateway bills.

So for their mission they were careful to choose an armored Five with a record of success. The previous crew in that ship had earned a "nova" science bonus in it, managing to come close enough to a recurring nova to get some good pictures, though not so close that they didn't live through the experience. They had collected a total of seven and a half million dollars in bonus money and had gone back to Earth, rejoicing. But before they left they gave their ship a name. They called it *Victory*.

When Sakyetsu and the others in his crew got to their destination they looked for the planet—or the star, or the Heechee artifact, or the object of any interesting sort—that might have been its target.

They were disappointed. There wasn't anything like that to be found anywhere around. There were stars in sight, sure. But the nearest of them was nearly eight light-years away. By all indications they had landed themselves in one of the most boringly empty regions of interstellar space in the galaxy. They could not find even a nearby gas cloud.

They didn't give up. They were experienced prospectors. They spent a week checking out every possibility. First, they made sure they hadn't missed a nearby star: with interferometry they could measure the apparent diameter of some of the brighter stars; by spectral analysis they could determine their types; combining the two gave them an estimate of distance.

Their first impression had been right. It was a pretty empty patch of sky they had landed in.

There was, to be sure, one really spectacular object in view—the word Marianna used was "glorious"—a globular cluster, with thousands of bright stars interweaving their orbits in a volume a few hundred light-years across. It was certainly spectacular. It dominated the sky. It was much nearer to them than any such object had ever been to a human eye before. But it was still at least a thousand light-years away.

A globular cluster is an inspiring sight. It was a long way from Sakyetsu and his ship *Victory*, but by the standards of Earthly astronomers that was nothing at all. Globular clusters live on the outer fringe of the galaxy. There aren't any in the crowded spiral-arm regions like the neighborhood of Earth. There are almost none less than twenty thousand light-years from Earth, and here was one a twentieth as far—and thus, by the law of inverse squares, four hundred times as bright. It was not an unusually large specimen, as globular clusters go; the big ones run upward of a million stars, and this one was nowhere near that. It was big enough to be exciting to look at, all the same.

But it was neither big enough nor near enough for *Victory*'s instruments to reveal any more than Earth's own orbiting observatories, with their far more powerful mirrors and optical systems, had seen long ago.

So there was very little chance that the instruments on *Victory* could earn them any kind of decent bonus. Still, those instruments were all they had. So the crew doggedly put them to work. They photographed the cluster in red light, blue light, ultraviolet light, and several bands of the infrared. They measured its radio flux in a thousand frequencies, and its gamma rays and X-rays. And then, one sleeping period, while only Hal M'Buna was awake at the instruments, he saw the thing that made the trip worthwhile.

His shout woke everybody up. "Something's eating the cluster!"

Marianna Morse was the first to get to the screens with him, but the whole crew flocked to see. The fuzzy circle of the cluster wasn't a circle anymore. An arc had been taken out of its lower rim. It looked like a cookie a child had bitten into.

But it wasn't a bite.

As they watched, they could see the differences. The stars of the cluster weren't disappearing. They were just, slowly, moving out of the way of—something.

"My God," Marianna whispered. "We're in orbit around a black hole."

Then they cursed the week they had wasted, because they knew what that meant. Big money! *A black hole.* One of the rarest objects (and, therefore, one of the most highly rewarded in science bonuses) in the observable universe—because black holes are, intrinsically, unobservable.

A black hole isn't "black," in the sense that a dinner jacket or the ink on a piece of paper is black. A black hole is a lot blacker than that. No human being has ever seen real *blackness*, because blackness is the absence of all light. It can't be seen. There is nothing to see. The blackest dye reflects a little light; a black hole reflects nothing at all. If you tried to illuminate it with the brightest searchlight in the universe—if you concentrated all the light of a quasar on it in a single beam—you would still see nothing. The tremendous gravitational force of the black hole would suck all that light in and it would never come out again. It can't.

It is a matter of escape velocity. The escape velocity from the Earth is seven miles a second; from a neutron star as much as 120,000 miles per second. But the escape velocity from a black hole is greater than the speed of light. The light doesn't "fall back" (as a rock thrown up from Earth at less than escape velocity will fall back to the ground). What happens to the light rays is that they are bent by the gravitational pull. The radiation simply circles the black hole, spiraling endlessly, never getting free.

And when a black hole passes in front of, say, a globular cluster, it doesn't hide the cluster. It simply bends the cluster's light around it.

If *Victory*'s crew had wasted seven days, they still had five days' worth of supplies left before they had to start back to Gateway. They used them all. They took readings on the black hole even when they couldn't see it . . . and when at last they got back to Gateway they found that one, just one, of their pictures had paid off.

They shared a five-hundred-thousand-dollar bonus simply for the pictures of the globular cluster. But the one picture that they hadn't even noticed when they took it—a split-second frame, taken automatically when no one happened to be watching the screen— showed what happened when the black hole occluded a bright B-4 star, a few hundred light-years away. That star hadn't moved up or down. By chance it had passed almost exactly behind the black hole. Its light had spread to surround the hole, like a halo; and that gave them a measure of the hole's size . . .

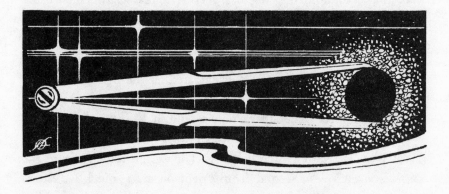

And then, long after they were back in Gateway, the research teams that studied their results awarded them another half a million, and the information that they were very lucky.

Marianna Morse had wondered about that: Why had the Heechee used an armored Five to visit this harmless object? Answer: It hadn't always been harmless.

Most black holes are not safe to visit. They pull in gases in accretion rings, and the acceleration of the gases as they fall produces a hell of radiation. Once this one had, but that was a long time ago. Now it had eaten all the gases in its neighborhood. There was nothing left to fall and so generate the synchrotron flux of energy that might fry even an armored Five if it lingered too long nearby . . . and so the crew of *Victory*, without knowing it at the time, had had an unexpected stroke of luck. They arrived at the neighborhood of their black hole after its lethal feeding frenzy had ended, and so they had come back alive.

In its first twenty years the Gateway Corporation handed out more than two hundred astronomical science bonuses, for a total of nearly one billion dollars. It paid off on double stars and supernova shells; it paid off on at least the first examples of every type of star there was.

There are nine members of the catalogue of star types, and they are easily remembered by the mnemonic "Pretty Woman, Oh, Be A Fine Girl, Kiss Me," which runs the gamut from youngest to longest-living stars. The stellar classes from A down to the dim, small, cool Ms didn't earn any special science bonuses unless there was something truly remarkable about them, because they were too common. The vast majority of stars were dim, small, and cool. Contrariwise, the Os and Bs were hot young stars, and they always got bonuses because they were so few. But the Gateway Corporation awarded double bonuses on the P and W classes: P for gas clouds just condensing into stars, W for the hot, frightening Wolf-Rayet type. These were new stars, often immense ones, that could not be approached safely within billions of miles.

All those lucky prospectors collected science bonuses. So did the ones who happened to find themselves near known objects, at least if they were the first to claim the rewards. Wolfgang Arretov was the first to arrive near the Sirius system, and Earthly astronomers were delighted. The stars Sirius A and B ("Bessel's satellite") had been studied intensively for centuries, because the primary star is so bright in Earthly skies. Arretov's data confirmed their deductions: Sirius A at 2.3 solar masses, B only about one—but a white dwarf with a surface temperature over twenty thousand degrees. Arretov got half a million for letting the astronomers know they had been right all along. Later, Sally Kissendorf got a hundred thousand for the first good pictures of the tiny (well—three solar masses, which is not *real* tiny; but just about invisible next to its huge primary) companion of Zeta Aurigae. She would have gotten more if the companion had happened to flare while she was nearby, but that might not have been worth her while, since it was very likely she could not have survived the experience. Matt Polofsky's picture of little Cygnus A only got him fifty thousand dollars, though—red dwarf stars simply weren't that interesting. Even well-studied nearby ones. And Rachel Morgenstern, with her husband and their three grown children, shared half a million for the Delta Cepheid shots. Cepheids aren't all that rare, but the Morgensterns happened to be there just when the star's surface layers were losing transparency through compression.

And then there were all the missions that wound up in Oort clouds.

Oort clouds are masses of comets that orbit a star very far out—the Oort in Earth's system doesn't get going until you're half a light-year from the Sun. There are *lots* of comets in your average Oort cloud. Trillions of them. They generally mass as much as the aggregate of a star's planets, and almost every star has an Oort.

They seemed to fascinate the Heechee.

In Gateway's first twenty years of operation, no fewer than eighty-five missions wound up in an Oort cloud and returned to tell of it.

That was a big disappointment to the prospectors involved, because the Gateway Corporation stopped paying bonuses for Oort data after the tenth such mission. So those prospectors who came back from an Oort complained a lot. They couldn't understand why the Heechee had targeted so many missions to the dumb things.

And, naturally, they had no idea how lucky they really were, because it was a long time before anyone found out that, for an astonishing reason, most Oort missions never got back to the Gateway asteroid at all.

That billion dollars in astronomical science bonuses was welcome enough to the prospectors who got a share of it. But, really, it was chicken feed. What the Gateway Corporation was formed for was *profit*. The prospectors had come to the asteroid for the same reason, and big profit didn't come from taking instrument readings on something millions of miles away. The big bucks came from finding a planet, and landing on it—and bringing back something that made money.

Neither the Gateway Corporation nor the individual prospectors had much choice about that. Making a profit was the basic rule of survival, and neither the prospectors nor the Corporation made the rules. Those rules were made by the nature of the world they came from.

PART FIVE

THE
HOME
PLANET

Homo sapiens evolved on the planet Earth, and the process of evolution made it certain that every human trait was custom-engineered to fit Earth's conditions, like a key in a lock. With three billion years of Darwinian selection to make the fit perfect, life on Earth should have been pretty nearly heaven for its human inhabitants.

It wasn't. Not anymore, for rich Earth was getting close to filing for bankruptcy. It had spent its wealth.

Oh, there were many millionaires on Earth. Billionaires, too; people with more money than they could spend, enough to hire a hundred servants, enough to own a county for a backyard, enough to pay for Full Medical insurance coverage, so that for all their long lives they would have at their command the most wonderful of all the wonderful medical, pharmaceutical, and surgical techniques to keep them healthy, and to make those lives very long. There were hundreds of thousands of the very rich, and many millions of the more or less well to do . . .

But there were ten billion others.

There were the ones who scratched out a living by farming on

156

Asian plains and African savannahs; they made a crop when rain fell and wars stayed away and marauding insect pests devoured some other countryside than their own, and when the crop failed they died. There were the ones who lived in the barricaded slums of the big cities (the word "ghetto" was no longer a metaphor), or the barrios outside Latin metropolises, or the teeming warrens of the urban areas of the Orient. These people worked when they could. They lived on charity when there was any charity to be had. They lived at the bottom of the food chain—rice and beans, yams and barley; or, if they had the money to pay for it, single-cell proteins from the fossil-fuel conversions of the food mines—and they were very likely to be hungry throughout every hour of every day of their lives. Which were short. The poor people couldn't afford the medical plans. If they were very lucky there might be a free clinic, or a cheap doctor, to hand out pills and take out an appendix. But when one of their organs wore out they had only two alternatives. They managed to get along without it; or they died. The poor people could never afford organ transplants. They were lucky if they weren't caught in a dark alley some night and themselves converted into transplants for some richer person, by some more desperate one.

So there were two kinds of human beings on Earth. If you owned a few thousand shares of PetroFood or Chemways you didn't lack for much—not even health, because then you could afford Full Medical. But if you didn't . . .

If you didn't, the next best thing was to have a job. Any kind of a job.

Having a job was a dream of Utopia for the billions who had none, but for those who did have employment their work was generally a demeaning kind of drudgery that drowned the spirit and damaged the health. The food mines employed many, dipping fossil fuels out of the ground and breeding edible single-cell protein creatures on their hydrocarbon content. But when you worked at a food mine you breathed those same hydrocarbons every day—it was like

living in a closed garage, with motors running all the time—and you probably died young. Factory work was better, a little, although the safest and most challenging parts of it were generally done by automatic machines for economic reasons; because they were more expensive to acquire, and to replace when damaged, than people. There was even domestic service as a possible career. But to be a servant in the homes of the wealthy was to be a slave, with a slave's intimate experience of luxury and plenty, and a slave's despair at ever attaining those things for himself.

Still, the ones who had even those jobs were lucky, for family agriculture was just a way of slowing down starvation, and in the developed world unemployment was terribly high. Especially in the cities. Especially for the young. So if you were one of the really rich, or even just one of the well-to-do, splurging on a trip to New York or Paris or Beijing, you usually saw the poor ones only when you walked out of your hotel, between police barricades, and into your waiting taxi.

You didn't have to do it that way. The police barricades were all one-way. If you chose to cross them the police would let you through. A grizzled old cop might try to warn you that going out among the crowds was a bad idea, if he happened to be charitably moved. But none of them would stop you if you insisted.

Then you were on your own. Which meant that you were immediately plunged into a noisy, smelly, dirty kind of unbarred zoo where you were immersed in a crowd of clamoring vendors: of drugs; of plastic reproductions of the Great Wall, the Eiffel Tower, or the New York Bubble; of handmade key charms and hand-carved trinkets; of guide services, or discount coupons to night clubs; of—very often—themselves. That was a scary experience for any member of the privileged classes encountering it for the first time. It wasn't necessarily very dangerous, though. The police wouldn't actually let them murder you or snatch your wallet—as long as you were in sight, anyway.

Quite often, the charging poor wouldn't harm you even if they

succeeded in luring you away from the police cordons, especially if
you offered them some less chancy way of making money from
you. But that was not guaranteed. Most of the poor people were
desperate.

For the rich, of course, the world was quite different. It always
is. The rich lived long, healthy lives with other people's organs
replacing any of their own that wore out. They lived those lives in
balmy climates under the domes of major cities, if they chose, or

cruising the warm and still-unpolluted southern seas, or even traveling in space for the pure joy of it. When there were wars (and
there often were, frequent though small—though quite large enough,
of course, to satisfy the people killed in them), the rich went elsewhere until the wars were over. They felt that was their due. After
all, they were the ones who paid the taxes—as much as they couldn't
avoid, anyway.

The main trouble with being rich was that not all of the poor people acquiesced in being poor. Quite a few tried to find ways to better themselves, and sometimes they did so violently.

Kidnapping became a growth industry in America again. So did extortion. You paid what they demanded, or out of hiding someone would shoot away your kneecap (or torch your house, or boobytrap your flyer, or poison your pets). Few in the solvent classes would send their children to school without a bodyguard anymore. That did have a useful side effect. As it turned out, it helped ease the unemployment situation, a little, as some millions of the extortionists put on uniforms and began drawing salaries to protect their employers against extortion.

And, of course, there was political terror, too. It flourished in the same soil that nurtured kidnapping and extortion, and there was even more of it. Among the apathetic majority of the landless and

the hungry, there were always a few who banded together to work the vengeance of the have-nots on the haves. Hostages were taken, officials were shot from ambush, aircraft were bombed out of the sky, reservoirs were poisoned, food supplies infected . . . oh, there were a thousand ingenious, injurious tricks the terror-wielders devised, and all of them devastating—at least, to those who had something to lose in the first place.

Nevertheless, in spite of all the fears and inconveniences, the haves had it made. And most other people didn't even have hope.

Then, into the life of this seething, overfull planet, along came Gateway.

For most of the ten billion people alive on the used-up planet of Earth, Gateway was an unexpected hope of paradise. Like the gold-rush miners of '49, like the hungry Irish fleeing their potato famine in the holds of immigrant ships, like the sodbusting pioneers of the American West and human emigrants everywhere, through all of history, the poverty-stricken billions were willing to take any risk for the sake of—well, wealth, if wealth could be had; but at least for a chance to feed and clothe and house their children.

Even the rich saw that this surprising new event might offer them a good chance to get even richer. That made for a serious problem, for a while. The national governments who had built the space rockets that first visited other planets and later supported the Gateway operation felt they were entitled to whatever profits came out of the Gateway discoveries. The rich people who owned the governments agreed. But they couldn't all own it, after all.

So there was a certain amount of buying and selling and horse-trading (and some pretty cutthroat wheeling and dealing, too, with the stakes as high as they were). Compromises were made. Bargains were struck; and out of the competing greeds of all the claimants to the limitless wealth that the galaxy promised came the just, or fairly just, invention of the Gateway Corporation.

Was Gateway a benefit to Earth's poor?

At first, not very much. It gave each of them a little hope—the hope of a lottery ticket, although few of them could raise the money even to buy that one-way ticket that might make them into winners. But it was a long time before any stay-at-home peasant or slum-dweller was a penny or a meal richer for anything the Heechee had left behind.

In fact, the knowledge that there were rich, empty planets out there was more tantalizing than useful to Earth's teeming billions. The livable planets were too far away. They could only be reached by faster-than-light travel. Although human beings actually improved on some Heechee space-travel techniques (using Lofstrom loops to get into orbit instead of Heechee landers, for instance, and thus sparing further damage to the acidified lakes and the ozone layer), no one had the slightest idea of how to build a Heechee ship—and the ships on Gateway were far too few and much too small to carry sizable migrant populations to the new planets.

So a few prospectors got rich, when they didn't get dead instead. A number of rich people got quickly richer. But most of the penniless billions stayed on Earth.

And in the cities like Calcutta, with its two hundred million paupers, and on the starved farms and paddies of Africa and the Orient, hunger remained a fact of life, and terrorism and poverty got worse instead of better.

PART SIX

OTHER WORLDS

As our teachers keep telling us, the longest journey begins with a single step. That first step for the Gateway asteroid—the first voyage of exploration any human being ever took in a Heechee spaceship—wasn't planned in advance. It wasn't even authorized. And it certainly wasn't prudent.

The name of the man who took that first trip into the unknown was Lieutenant Senior Grade Ernest T. Kaplan. He was a marine officer from the U.S. Space Navy cruiser *Roanoke*. Kaplan wasn't a scientist. He was so far from being a scientist that he had been given strict orders not to touch anything, but *anything*, on the Gateway asteroid. The only reason he was on the asteroid in the first place was that he had been ordered there as a guard, to keep anyone else from touching anything while the scientists who came hurrying up from Earth tried to figure out just what the devil they had here.

But Kaplan had a mind full of itchy curiosity, and what's more, he had access to the parked ships. And one day, for lack of anything better to do, he sat down in the one ship that happened to have been equipped with food lockers and air and water tanks, just in case anyone got the locks closed and was trapped inside. Kaplan thought for a while about old Sylvester Macklin. Just for the fun of it, he practiced opening and closing the locks a few times. Then he played with the knurled wheels for a while, watching the changing colors.

Then he squeezed the funny-looking little thing at the base.

That was what later, more expert pilots would call "the launch teat," and as soon as he squeezed it Lieutenant Senior Grade Kaplan became the second human being to fly a Heechee ship. He was *gone*.

Ninety-seven days later he was back at the Gateway asteroid.

It was a miracle that he'd managed to return; it was even a bigger miracle that he was still alive. The supplies in the ship had been meant to last for a few days, not for months. For drinking water he had been reduced to catching the condensation from his own sweat and emanations as it beaded the lander port. For the last five weeks he hadn't eaten anything at all. He was scrawny and filthy and half out of his mind . . .

But he had *been there*. His ship had orbited a planet far out from a small, reddish star; a planet that had so little light that it seemed only grayish, with swirling yellow clouds—a little the way Jupiter or Saturn or Uranus might have appeared, if their orbits had been as far from the Sun as the twilit Pluto.

The first reaction of the United States government was to court-martial him. He certainly deserved it. He even expected it.

But before the court was convened the news services carried the word that the Brazilian parliament, carried away at the thought of sharing in the exploration of the galaxy, had voted Kaplan a million-dollar cash bonus. Then the Soviets not only made him an honorary citizen but invited him to Moscow to receive the Order of Lenin. The dam had burst. Every talk show on every television network in the world was begging him to be a guest.

You couldn't court-martial a hero.

So the American president jumped Lieutenant Kaplan to full colonel and then to general, in the same orders that grounded Colonel (or General) Kaplan forever. Then the president called all the spacefaring nations together to decide just how to handle this situation.

The result was the Gateway Corporation.

Colonel Kaplan, like everyone before him, had failed to make one vital discovery, and that was that each one of the Heechee ships was actually two ships. Part One was the interstellar vessel that traveled faster than light to a programmed destination. Part Two was the smaller, simpler landing craft that nestled into the base of the ship itself.

The interstellar ships themselves, with their unreproducible faster-than-light drives, were totally beyond the understanding of human scientists. It was a long time before any Earth person knew how they worked. Those who tried too hard to find out generally died because their drive engines blew up. The landers were much simpler. Basically, they were ordinary rockets. True, the guidance system was Heechee, but fortunately for the Gateway prospectors the controls turned out to be even simpler to operate than the faster-than-light vessels. The prospectors could use the lander successfully, even if they didn't know exactly how it worked, just as any average seventeen-year-old can learn to drive a car without any comprehension of the geometry of steering linkages or gear chains.

So when any Gateway prospector came out of FTL drive and found himself in the vicinity of an interesting-looking planet, he could use the lander for the purpose for which it was designed: to go down to the surface of the planet and see what it had to offer.

That was what Gateway was all about.

The planets were where you had to go, because they were the most likely places to look for the kind of precious thing the prospector could bring back and turn in to make his fortune—and, naturally, to add to the Corporation's.

It was easy to describe the kind of planets they were looking for. They were looking for another Earth. Or something enough like Earth, anyway, to support some form of organic life, because inorganic processes hardly ever produced anything worth the carrying space it took to bring it home.

The most disappointing planets were the closest. When the Heechee came to Earth's solar system they gave it a good looking-over, and some of the ships on the Gateway asteroid reflected that. They still had stored navigation codes for places so near that human beings could have visited them on their own—if they wanted to. Some of them in fact had already been reached by the crude human rockets—places like Venus, the Moon, Mars's south polar ice cap. Some were hardly worth the trouble, like Saturn's moon, Dione.

The prospectors were after bigger game than that. They wanted planets no man or woman had ever seen. They found a bewildering array of them.

The planets they reached in the Magic Mystery Bus Rides came in all shapes and sizes. There were two basic types. There were the orbiting rocks (like Earth; solid and landable-on), and then there were the would-be stars (like Jupiter; the gas giants, that were just a bit too small to start nuclear fusion in their cores and turn themselves into suns). No Gateway prospector ever landed on a gas giant, of course. They had nothing solid enough to land on. (That was a pity, for a few of them were interesting anyway . . . but that's another story.)

It was the orbiting rocks that were prospected as vigorously as a few thousand scared, hurried human beings could explore them. There were plenty of the solid planets. Most of them had no apparent life at all, unfortunately. They were too far from their sun, so they were eternally frozen, or they were too close, so they were as scorched as the planet Mercury. Many of them had too little atmosphere (or none at all), like Mars (or the Moon). Some of them had satellites of their own, like the Earth's Moon. Some of the target objects *were* satellites, but big ones, big enough to retain atmospheres and to land on.

There were something over two hundred billion stars in our own galaxy, and a hellish lot of them possessed planets of one kind or another. Even the Heechee ships weren't programmed to set a course for all the possible planets to explore. There were hardly course settings for one planet in a hundred thousand, in fact. Still, that left plenty for the Gateway prospectors to visit—many more of them than a few thousand men and women could reach in the course of a few dozen years.

So the first discovery the Gateway prospectors made was that there were plenty of planets to choose from. Human astronomers were glad to know that, because they'd always wondered, and the Corporation didn't even have to pay a discovery bonus to find it out: all they had to do was add up the findings of the returning explorers. It developed that binary stars didn't ordinarily have planets. Solitary stars, on the other hand, generally did. Astronomers thought the reason for that probably had something to do with conserving rotational velocity. When two stars condensed together out of a single gas cloud they seemed to take care of each other's excess rotational energy. Bachelor stars apparently had to dissipate it on smaller satellites.

Hardly any of the planets were really Earth-like, though.

There were a lot of tests for that sort of thing that could be applied from a considerable distance. Temperature sensing, for one. Organic life didn't seem to develop except where water could exist in its liquid phase, which was to say in the narrow, 100-degree band between about 270 and 370 Kelvin. At lower temperatures the stuff was useless ice. At higher ones water wasn't usually there at all, because the heat vaporized it and the sunlight—from whatever sun was nearby—split the hydrogen out of the water molecule and it was lost into space.

That meant that each star had a quite narrow area of possible planetary orbits that might be worth investigating. As planets didn't care whether or not they were going to be hospitable to life when they were condensing out of the interstellar gases, most of them took orbits inside that life zone, or in the cold spaces outside it.

Most alien life, like most Earthly life, was based on the chemistry of the carbon atoms. Carbon was the best of all possible elements for forming useful long-chain compounds, and happily it is so frequently found that it is the fourth most common element in the universe. Most alien life had something like DNA, too. That wasn't for any panspermian reason, but simply because systems like DNA provided a cheap and efficient way for organisms to replicate themselves.

So most living things followed certain basic guidelines. That was probably because they all started in pretty much the same way, since there is a timetable to the development of life. The first step is just chemistry: inorganic chemicals get forced to react with each other, under the spur of some sort of externally supplied energy—usually the light from their nearby star. Then crude, single-celled little things appear. These are only factories whose raw materials are the other inorganic chemicals in the soup that surrounds them. They, too, use the energy of sunlight (or whatever) to process the inorganic chemicals into more of themselves, and that's about all they do for a living. Since they are photosynthetic, you might call them plants.

Then these primitive "plants" themselves turn out to be pretty rich sources of assimilable chemicals. Since they've gone to the trouble of concentrating the more appetizing inorganic compounds into a preprocessed form, it is only a question of time until some of them learn a new diet. These new ones don't eat the raw materials of the environment. They eat their own weaker, more primitive cousins. Call this new batch of creatures "animals." The first animals aren't usually much. They consist of a mouth at one end, an anus at the other, and some sort of processing system in between. That's all they are. But then, that's all they need to be to feast on their neighbors.

Then things get more complicated.

Evolution begins to happen. The fittest survive, pretty much the way Charles Darwin figured it out as he fondled his captive finches on board the *Beagle*. The plants go on making appetizing chemicals for the animals to feast on, and the animals go on feasting on the plants and on each other—but some plants accidentally develop traits that give their predators trouble, and so those plants survive; and some animals learn tricks to get around those defenses. Later generations of animals develop senses to locate their prey more efficiently, and musculatures to catch it, and ultimately complex behavioral systems (like the web of a spider or the stalking of a great cat) that make their predation more and more successful. (Then, of course, the plants, or the herbivores, or the less successful predators begin to develop defense mechanisms of their own: the poisons in a shrub's leaf, the quills of a porcupine, the fleet legs of a gazelle.) The competition never stops getting more intense, and more sophisticated on all parts—until, finally, some of the creatures become "intelligent." But they take a lot longer to evolve . . . and it took the Gateway prospectors a lot longer to find any of them, too.

In the myriad worlds that the Heechee had explored—and to which the human Gateway prospectors followed them hundreds of thousands of years later—all those basics of the evolution of life were played out a thousand times, with a thousand variations. The variations were sometimes quite surprising. For instance, Earthly plants have one conspicuous trait in common: they don't move. But there wasn't any reason why that trait had to be universal, and in fact it wasn't. The Gateway prospectors found bushes that rolled from place to place, setting roots down to one side and pulling them up on the other, like slow-motion tumbleweeds as they sought the richest soils and the best access to groundwater and the surest sunlight. Then, too, Earthly animals don't normally bother with photosynthesis. But in the seas of other worlds there were things like jellyfish that floated to the surface by day to generate their own hydrocarbons from the sun and the air, and then sank down to feast on algal things at night. Earthly corals stay in one place. Prospectors found some unearthly ones—or, at least, some unearthly things that looked more or less like corals—that flew apart into their component little animals when the coast was clear, to eat and mate, and then returned to form collective rockhard fortresses when the prowling marine predators approached.

Most of these things were useless to any prospector whose big interest was in making a fortune. A few were not. There was one good feature to finding an organism that was worth something, and that was that it was an easy import. You didn't have to bring tons of material back to Gateway. All you had to do was bring enough of some plant or animal back to breed others back on Earth, since living things were glad to reproduce themselves for you anywhere.

The zoos of Earth began to expand, and so did Earth's aquaria, and its pet stores. Every fashionable family was sure to own its exotic windowbox of alien ferns, or its furry little pet from the planet of some other star.

Before the Gateway prospectors could make an honest buck in the pet trade, though, they had to find the living things in the first place. That wasn't easy. Even when life was apparently possible, sometimes it was there, and sometimes it was not. The way to check for that was to look for chemical signatures in the atmosphere. (Oh, yes, the hopefully life-bearing planet had to possess an atmosphere, too, but that wasn't a serious constraint. Most planets in the habitable zone did.) If the atmosphere turned out to contain reactive gases that hadn't reacted—say, if it held free oxygen, with reducing substances like carbon or iron somewhere availably around—then it stood to reason that something must be continually replenishing those gases. That something was probably, in some sense, alive.

(Later on the prospectors found there were exceptions to these simple rules . . . but not many.)

The very first planet that turned out to have living things on it was a solid ten when studied from orbit. Almost everything was there: blue skies, blue seas, fleecy white clouds and plenty of oxygen—meaning some antientropic (i.e., living) thing to keep it that way.

Prospectors Anatol and Sherba Mirsky and their partner, Leonie Tilden, slapped each other's backs in exultation as they prepared to land. It was their first mission—and they'd hit the jackpot right away.

Naturally they celebrated. They opened the one bottle of wine they'd brought along. Ceremonially they made a recording announcing their discovery, punctuating it with the pop of the wine cork. They called the planet New Earth.

Everything was going their way. They even thought it likely that they could figure out just where they were in the galaxy (a kind of knowledge usually hidden from the early Gateway prospectors, because there weren't any road signs on the way). But they had spotted the Magellanic Clouds in one direction and the Andromeda Nebula in another, and in still a third direction there was a tight, bright cluster that they were nearly sure was the Pleiades.

The celebration was a bit premature. It had not occurred to them that one interesting color was missing in their view of New Earth from space, and that color was green.

When Sherba Mirsky and Leonie Tilden went down to the surface of New Earth in the lander, what they landed on was bare rock. Nothing grew there. Nothing moved. Nothing flew in the sky. There were no flowering plants. There were no plants at all, at their elevation; there wasn't any soil for them to grow in. Soil hadn't reached those parts of the world yet.

It was only one more disappointment to find that there wasn't much oxygen in its air, either—enough for a qualitative determination from orbit, yes, but nowhere near enough to breathe. For, although there certainly was life on New Earth, there just wasn't much of it yet. Most of what there was lived in the coastal shallows, with a few hardy adventurers just making a start in colonizing the shores—simple prokaryotic and eukaryotic denizens of the sludgy seas, with a few scraggly, mossy things that had struggled out onto the littoral.

The trouble with New Earth was that it was a lot too new. It would take a billion years or so to get really interesting—or to pay Tilden, the Mirskys, and the Gateway Corporation back for the trouble of looking it over.

Although it was planets that offered profits, planets were also the places where it was easiest to get killed. As long as a Gateway prospector stayed inside his ship he was well protected against most of the dangers of star wandering. It was when he landed that he exposed himself to unknown environments . . . and often very hostile ones.

For example, there was—

MISSION *PRETTY POISON*

A fifty-year-old Venezuelan named Juan Mendoza Santamaria was the first Gateway prospector to discover a really nice-looking planet. It had taken him forty-three days to get there, all alone in a One. That was well within his margins. He was not likely to run out of air, food, or water. What he worried about running out of was money. Mendoza had spent the last of his credits on a farewell party before he left the asteroid. If he came back empty-handed to Gateway his future was bleak. So he crossed himself and whispered a prayer of gratitude as he stepped out of his lander onto the alien soil.

He was grateful, but he wasn't stupid. Therefore he was also cautious. Mendoza knew very well that if anything went wrong he was in serious trouble. There was no one within many light-years who could help him—in fact, there wasn't anybody, anywhere, who even knew where he was. So he wore his space suit at all times on the surface of the planet, and that turned out to be very fortunate for Juan Mendoza.

The planet didn't look threatening at all. The plants were an odd shade of orange, the distant trees (or were they simply very tall grasses?) looked harmless, and there were no obviously threatening large animals. On the other hand, there wasn't much to be seen that looked immediately profitable, either. There weren't any signs of civilization—no great abandoned cities, no friendly alien intelligences to welcome him, no Heechee artifacts lying about waiting to be picked up. There wasn't even any kind of metallic structure, natural or otherwise, on the surface large enough to be detected by his lander's sensors as he came down. But, Mendoza reassured himself, the fact that there was any kind of life ought to be worth at least a science bonus. He identified both "plant" and "animal" life—

at least some of the things moved, and some of them were firmly rooted in the soil.

He took some samples of the plants, though they weren't impressive. He trekked painfully over to the "trees" and found that they were soft-bodied, like mushrooms. There weren't any large ferns or true grasses; but there was a kind of fuzzy moss that covered most of the soil, and there were things that moved on it. None of the moving things were very big. The largest life form Mendoza encountered was an "arthropod" about the size of his palm. The little beasts moved about in little herds, feeding on smaller beetly and buggy things, and they were covered with a dense "fur" of glassy white spicules, which made them look like herds of tiny sheep. Mendoza felt almost guilty as he trapped a few of the pretty little creatures, killed them, and put them, with samples of the smaller creatures they preyed on, in the sterile containers that would go back to Gateway.

There wasn't anything else worth transporting. What the planet had that was really worthwhile was beauty. It had a lot of that.

It was quite near—Mendoza estimated thirty or forty light-years—a bright, active gas cloud that he thought might be the Orion Nebula. (It wasn't, but like the one in Orion it was a nursery for bright young stars.) Mendoza happened to land in the right season of the year to appreciate it best, for as the planet's sun set on one horizon the nebula rose on the other. It came to fill the entire night sky, like a luminous, sea-green tapestry laced with diamonds, edged in glowing royal maroon. The "diamonds"—the brightest stars within the nebula—were orders of magnitude brighter even than Venus or Jupiter as seen from Earth, nearly as bright as Earth's full Moon. But they were point sources, not disks like the Moon, and they were almost painful to look upon.

It was the beauty that struck Mendoza. He was not an articulate man. When he got back and filed his report he referred to the planet as "a pretty place," and so it was logged in the Gateway atlases as "Pretty Place."

Mendoza got what he was after: a two-million-dollar science bonus for finding the planet at all, and the promise of a royalty share on whatever subsequent missions might discover on Pretty Place. That could have turned out to be really serious money. According to Gateway rules, if the planet was colonizable Mendoza would be collecting money from it for the rest of his life.

Almost at once two other missions, both Fives, copied his settings and made the same trip.

That was when they changed the name to Pretty Poison.

The follow-up parties were not as cautious as Mendoza. They didn't keep their space suits on. They didn't have the natural protections that had been developed by Pretty Poison's own fauna, either. The local life had evolved to meet a real challenge; those furry silicon spikes were not for ornament. They were armor.

It was a pity Mendoza hadn't completed his radiation checks, because those bright young stars in the nebula were not radiating visible light alone. They were powerful sources of ionizing radiation and hard ultraviolets. Four of the ten explorers came down with critical sunburn before they began to show signs of something worse. All of them, by the time they got back to Gateway, required total blood replacement, and two of them died anyway.

It was a good thing that Mendoza was a prudent man. He hadn't spent his two million in wild carouse, expecting the vast royalties that might come as his percentage of all that colonizing his planet would bring about. The planet could not be inhabited by human beings. The royalties never came.

MISSION *BURNOUT*

Of the nearly thousand Heechee vessels found on Gateway, only a few dozen were armored, and most of those were Fives. An armored Three was a rarity, and when the crew of Felicia Monsanto, Greg Running Wolf, and Daniel Pursy set out in one they knew there was a certain element of danger; its course setting might take them to some really nasty place.

But when they came out of FTL and looked around they had a moment of total rapture. The star they were near was quite sunlike, a G-2 the same size as Earth's Sol; they were orbiting a planet within the livable zone from the star, and their detectors showed Heechee metal in large quantities!

The biggest concentration was not on the planet. It was an asteroid in an out-of-ecliptic orbit—a lot like Gateway—and it *had* to be another of those abandoned parking garages for Heechee ships! When they approached it they saw that the guess was correct . . .

But they also saw that the asteroid was empty. There were no ships. There were no artifacts at all. It was riddled with tunnels, just like Gateway, but the tunnels were vacant. Worse than that, the whole asteroid seemed in very bad shape, as though it were far older, and had had a far harder life, than Gateway itself.

That puzzle cleared itself up when, with the last of their resources, two of the crew ventured down to the planet itself.

It had been a living planet once. It had life now, in fact, but in scant numbers and only in its seas—algae and sea-bottom invertebrates, nothing more. Somehow or other the planet had been seared and ravaged . . . and the culprit was in view.

Six and a half light-years away from that system they discovered a neutron star. Like most neutron stars, it was a pulsar, but as their ship was nowhere near its axis of radiation they could hardly detect its jets. But it was a radio source, and their instruments showed that it was there, the remnant of a supernova.

The rest of the story the experts on Gateway filled in for them when they returned. That solar system had been visited by the Heechee, but it was in a bad neighborhood. After the Heechee left— probably knowing what was about to happen—the supernova exploded. The planet had been baked. Its gases had been driven off, and most of its seas boiled away. As the hellish heat died away a thin new atmosphere was cooked out of the planet's crust, and the remaining water vapor had come down in incredible torrents of rain, scouring away mountain valleys, burying plains in silt, leaving nothing . . . and all of that had happened hundreds of thousands of years before.

Monsanto, Running Wolf, and Pursy got a science bonus for their mission—a small one, a hundred and sixty thousand dollars to be divided among the three of them.

By Gateway standards, that wasn't serious money. It was enough to pay their bills on Gateway for a few extra weeks. It was not nearly enough to retire on. All three of them shipped out again as soon as they found another berth, and from their next voyage none of them ever returned.

Probably the Gateway prospectors should have taken it for granted that hospitable, Earth-like planets were bound to be a lot rarer than malignant ones. Their own solar system made that much clear. Anyway, all those years of listening to Project Ozma radio signals should have taught them that much.

What they found out was that there was a myriad different kinds of hostile environments. There was Eta Carina Seven; it was the right size, it had air, it even had water—when it wasn't frozen, anyway. But Eta Carina Seven had a highly eccentric orbit. It was pretty well iced over, though still on its way to its frigid aphelion, and there were terrible storms. One lander never came back at all. Three of the others were damaged, or lost at least one crew member.

Mendoza was not the only one to find a planet that looked nice but turned out to be poison. One pleasing-looking planet was well vegetated, but the vegetation was all toxicodendrons. They were far worse than Earth's poison ivy. The slightest touch meant blisters, agonizing itching pain, and anaphylactic shock. On the first mission to it everyone who landed on its surface died of allergic reactions, and only the crew member who stayed with the ship in orbit was able to get back to Gateway.

But once in a while—oh, *very* seldom—there was a good one.

The happiest of all, in the first decade of Gateway's operation, was the mission of Margaret Brisch, usually called "Peggy."

Peggy Brisch went out in a One. She found what was really another Earth. In fact, in some ways it was nicer than Earth ever was. Not only were there no toxicodendrons to kill anyone who touched, or any nearby star with lethal radiation, there were not even any large, dangerous animals.

There was only one thing wrong with Peggy's Planet. It would have been an ideal place to take Earth's overflow population, if only it hadn't been located a good nineteen hundred light-years away.

There was no way to get to it except on a Heechee ship. And the largest Heechee ship carried only five people.

The colonization of Peggy's Planet would have to wait.

First and last, the Gateway prospectors found more than two hundred planets with significant life. It drove the taxonomists happily crazy. Generations of doctoral candidates had dissertation material that could not fail to win their degrees, and hard work simply to find names for the thirty or forty million new species the prospectors found for them.

They didn't have that many names to spare, of course. The best they could do was assign classification numbers and note the descriptions. There was no hope of establishing genera or even families, although all the descriptions were fed into the databanks and a lot of computer time went into trying to discover relationships. The best descriptions were generic; DNA, or something like it, was pretty nearly universal. The next best were morphological. Most living things on Earth share such common architectural features as the rod (indispensable for limbs and bones in general) and the cylinder (internal organs, torsos, and so on), because they provide the most strength and carrying capacity you can get for the money. For the same reasons, so did most of the galaxy's bestiary. Not always, though. Arcangelo Pelieri's crew found a mute world, full of soft-bodied things that had never developed bones or chitin, soundless as earthworms or jellyfish. Opal Cudwallader reached a planet where, the scientists deduced, repeated extinctions had kept knocking off land animals as they developed. Its principal creature, like Earthly pinnipeds and cetaceans, was a former land-dweller returned to the sea, and nearly everything else was related. It was as though Darwin's finches had colonized an entire planet.

And so on and so on, until the explorers began to think they had found every possible variation on water-based, oxygen-breathing life.

Perhaps they almost had.

But then they found the Sluggards—the same race the Heechee had known as the Slow Swimmers—and took another look at the hitherto unimagined possible flora and fauna of the gas giants.

So they had been wrong in their basic assumption that life required the chemistry of a solid planet to evolve. That was a shock to their scientists . . . but not nearly the shock that came a bit later, when they discovered that life didn't require chemistry at all.

PART SEVEN

HEECHEE
TREASURES

Planets were nice, and pictures of stars were nice, but what everyone really wanted were some more samples of Heechee technology. There wasn't any doubt that there was some of the stuff waiting to be found—somewhere. The ships proved that. The little morsels picked up in the tunnels of Venus had proved it even earlier. But they just whetted the human appetite for more of these wonders.

Fourteen months after the program officially started, a mission got lucky.

Their ship was what was generally called a Five, but the system had not yet begun to operate in a standardized way. This time only four volunteers went along. They were officially chosen by the four Earth powers that had established the Gateway Corporation (the Martians took an interest later), and so they were an American, a Chinese, a Soviet, and a Brazilian. They had learned from the experience of Colonel Kaplan and others who had gone before. They brought along enough food, water, and oxygen to last them for six months; they were taking no chances this time.

As it happened, they didn't need all those provisions. Their ship brought them back in forty-nine days, and they didn't come back empty-handed.

Their destination had turned out to be an orbit around a planet about the size of the Earth. They had managed to make the lander work, and three of them had actually used it to set foot on the surface of the planet.

For the first time in human history, men walked on the surface of a heavenly body that was not part of the Sun's entourage.

First impressions were a bit disappointing. The four-power party discovered quickly enough that the planet had had some bad times. Its surface was seared, as though by great heat, and parts of it made their radiation detectors squeal. They knew they could not stay there long. But a mile or less from the lander, down a barren slope from the mountaintop mesa where they had landed, they found some rock and metal formations that looked artificial, and poking around them they dug up three items they thought worth bringing home. One was a flat tile with a triangular design still visible on its

glazed surface. The second was a ceramic object about the size of a cigar, with thread markings—a bolt? The third was a yard-long metal cylinder, made of chromium and pierced with a couple of holes; it could have been a musical instrument, or part of a machine—even a Hilsch tube.

Whatever they were, they were *artifacts*.

When the four-power crew proudly displayed their trophies back on the Gateway asteroid, they created an immense stir. None of the three looked like a major technological breakthrough. Nevertheless, if such things could be found, then there were certainly others—and no doubt things that would be of a lot more practical value.

That was when the interstellar gold rush began in earnest.

It was a long time before anyone got that lucky again. Overall, the statistics on missions out of the Gateway asteroid showed that four out of five trips came back with nothing to show but some pictures and instrument readings. Fifteen percent never came back at all. It was only one ship out of twenty that brought back any tangible piece of Heechee technology, and most of those things were only curiosities—but the very few that were more than curiosities were treasures beyond price.

They were few and far between, to be sure. The exploration of Venus had shown that was probable, for in all the hundreds of miles of Heechee tunnels under the surface of the planet Venus no more than a dozen gadgets had been found.

To be sure, some of those meant big profits for those who learned to copy them. The anisokinetic punch was a marvel. Hammer it on one end, and the force of the blow came out at the side. What was even more marvelous was that scientists managed to figure out how it worked, and its principle had applications in every area of construction, manufacture, and even home repair. The fire-pearls were a mystery. So were the so-called prayer fans.

Then, of course, humans reached the Gateway asteroid, and that fleet of ships was the biggest treasure trove of all. But all there was on the asteroid were the ships themselves. The ships were empty of anything but their operating gear. The whole asteroid was empty, almost surgically clean ... as though the Heechee had deliberately left the ships but removed everything else that could be of value.

Over a period of twenty years and more the Gateway explorers went out to seek whatever could be found. They came back with pictures and stories, and kinds of living things and minerals; but of Heechee artifacts they found very few.

That was why so many Gateway prospectors died poor—or just died.

MISSION *TOOLBOX*

Some also died rich, without knowing they had become rich. That was the case in one of the biggest finds. Unfortunately, it did three of its five discoverers little good, because they did not survive the trip.

The mission started with three Austrians, two brothers and an uncle, using the last of an inheritance to pay their way to Gateway. They were determined to ship out only in an armored ship. As the only such vessel available was a Five, at the last minute they recruited a South American, Manuel de los Fintas, and an American, Sheri Loffat, to go with them.

They reached a planet; they landed on the planet; they found nothing much there. But their instruments showed Heechee metal somewhere around, and they tracked it down.

It was a lander. It had been abandoned there, heaven knew when. But it was not empty.

The biggest thing they found in the lander was a stack of Heechee metal hexagonal boxes, not more than half a meter across and less than half that tall, weight twenty-three kilograms. They were

tools. Some of the items were familiar, and useless as far as anyone had been able to tell: almost a dozen little prayer fans of the kind that littered so many Heechee tunnels and artifacts. But there were also things like screwdrivers but with flexible shafts; things like socket wrenches but made out of some soft material; things that resembled electrical test probes but turned out to be spare parts for other Heechee machines.

It was a grand success. They wound up millionaires—or, at least, the survivors did.

That find was lying right on the surface of the planet. But before long the Gateway prospectors learned that planet surfaces were not the most likely places to look for examples of Heechee treasures. *Under* the surface was much, much richer.

One thing was clear early on about the vanished Heechee: they liked tunnels. The Heechee tunnels that honeycombed parts of the planet Venus weren't unique. As explorations retraced the old interstellar trails they found examples of them everywhere the Heechee had gone. The inside of the Gateway asteroid was a maze of tunnels; so were the "other Gateways" that turned up as the explo-

rations progressed. Nearly every planet the Heechee had left any signs on at all had tunnels dug into it, lined with Heechee metal. Where the surface conditions were unpleasant (as on Venus), the tunnels were extensive and complex. But even so fair a world as Peggy's Planet had a few of them. The anthropologically trained scientists called Heecheeologists, trying passionately to figure out what these vanished people were like, supposed that they came from a burrowing race, like gophers, rather than an arboreal one, like people. The Heecheeologists turned out to be right ... but it was a long time before any of them were sure of it.

All the tunnels looked pretty much alike. They were lined with a dense, hard, metallic substance that glowed in the dark: it was called Heechee metal. In the first tunnels humans encountered, on Venus and on the Gateway asteroid itself, the glow was a pale blue. Blue was by far the commonest of Heechee-metal colors, but inside the Heechee ships there were some parts that were made of a golden Heechee metal, and later on the explorers found Heechee metal that glowed red or green.

No one really knew why Heechee metal came in different colors. The Heecheeologists were not much help. All they could tell about the occasional variation in the color of Heechee metal was that it seemed clear that the tunnels of bluish metal were generally the ones poorest in Heechee artifacts: Gold, red, and green almost always had more treasures to be found by the explorers.

Of course, until men and women began to learn how to explore the galaxy in the Heechee ships, they were limited to the blue-glowing tunnels of Gateway and Venus. And in them the treasures to be found were sparse, though sometimes of great value. In the tunnels found on the most productive planets, the metal walls started out blue, and then became another color just where the largest collections of useful tools were located. No one knew why ... but then, no one knew much about the Heechee at all, just then.

MISSION *HEATER*

Wu Fengtse had chosen to ship out in a One. That had its advantages, and its faults. The biggest advantage was that if there was nothing to land on, and the only reward would be some kind of science bonus for observations, he could keep it all himself.

It didn't happen that way, though. When he came out of FTL drive, he found himself in orbit around a more or less Earth-type planet.

So Wu had to face the problem of every single prospector: If he took his lander down to the surface of the planet, no one would be left in the ship. If anything happened to him on the surface, no one would be there to rescue him. He was completely on his own.

His other problem was that "Earth-type" was only a very approximate description of the world he had to explore. "Earth-type" meant that the planet was about the right size, and that it had an atmosphere and a temperature range that permitted water vapor in the air, liquid water in its shallow seas, and frozen water on its colder parts. It wasn't heaven, though. Its colder parts included nearly all of the planet. Its best zone was around the equator, and that was not much unlike Labrador.

If there ever had been anything on any other part of its surface, it was now covered with thousands of feet of ice. There was no point in landing on a glacier; Wu had no way of digging down to whatever lay under it. After a lot of searching Wu found a bare outcropping of rock and landed there. By then he wasn't very optimistic anymore. The environment did not look promising—but his instruments gave him better news than he had expected.

There was a tunnel.

Wu had practiced tunnel entry. He even had the necessary equipment. Sweating the big power drills into place and erecting the bubble shelter that would protect it from the outside air took all of his strength, and enough time to use up the bulk of his supplies. But he got in.

It was a blue-lined tunnel.

That was discouraging, but as he moved along it he caught glimpses of other colors. When he got to a red segment he found a huge machine—later on, experts decided from his description that it had been a tunnel digger—but he didn't have the strength to lift it, or the equipment (or the courage, for that matter) to try to hack pieces off it. In the green part of the tunnel were bolts of what Wu first took to be cloth but turned out to be the crystalline sheeting the "prayer fans" were made of. In the gold was—the gold.

There were stacks and stacks of little hexagonal Heechee-metal boxes, all sealed. All heavy.

Wu couldn't carry them all, and his energy was running out. He managed to get two of them back to the lander and then took off, with every intention of coming back in a Five.

Unfortunately, when he was safely back on Gateway it turned out that no Five would accept the program that had brought him there. Neither would any of the Threes or Ones that were lying in their docks, waiting for crews.

It seemed that only the One he had found the planet in would take him back.

That didn't work, either. Before he could requisition it and ship out again someone else had taken his One—on a one-way trip.

All Wu had, then, was the two little boxes, but it was their contents that bought him a home in Shensi province. One of them contained heater coils. They weren't operating, but they were close enough to working condition so that human scientists managed to tinker them going. (Later on better and bigger ones were found on Peggy's Planet, but Wu's were still the first.) The other box contained a set of gauges for measuring microwave flux.

Scientists puzzled over the gauges very diligently, but they asked the wrong questions. What they labored to ascertain was how they worked. It did not occur to any of them, just then, to wonder *why* the Heechee were so curious about millimeter microwave flux. If it

191

had it might have saved a lot of people a lot of unnecessary confusion.

It was in a tunnel on an otherwise unprepossessing planet that one prospector found the first specimen of the Heechee tunneling machine. It was in a tunnel on the Luna-like satellite of a distant gas giant planet that another found the "camera" that the so-called "fire-pearls" served as "film." And it was in a tunnel that Vitaly Klemenkov found the little device that sparked a whole new industry—and earned him only a pittance.

Klemenkov's is a kind of hard-luck story. What he found was what human scientists came to call a "piezophone." Its main operating part was a diaphragm made out of the same material as the "blood-diamonds" that had littered the tunnel of Venus and many others. The material was piezoelectric: when squeezed it produced an electric current, and vice versa. Of course, there were plenty of blood-diamonds around, though no one had known before Klemenkov that they were basically raw material for piezoelectric devices. Klemenkov had visions of untold riches. Unfortunately, the main communications laboratories on Earth, subsidiaries of the cable and telephone and satellite corporations, developed the Heechee model into something they could manufacture themselves. Klemenkov took it to court, naturally—but who could fight the lawyers of the biggest corporations in the world? So he settled for a small royalty—hardly more, in fact, than an average emperor's income.

There was one other splendidly productive variety of place to find Heechee treasures. But no one knew that at first, although if they had thought of the example of Gateway itself they might have deduced it, and certainly no one knew that these rich lodes were, actually, traps. A woman named Patricia Bover was the first Gateway prospector to report finding one—and, as was so often the case, it did her little good.

MISSION *FOOD FACTORY*

Patricia Bover set out in a One. She had no idea where she was going. She was pleased that it was a relatively short trip—turnaround in seven days, destination in fourteen—and astonished when her instruments told her that the tiny, distant star that was the nearest to her was actually the old familiar Sun.

She was in the Oort cloud of comets, far beyond the orbit of Pluto, and she was docking on what was clearly a Heechee artifact. A big one: it was eight hundred feet long, she estimated, and it was like nothing anyone had ever before reported finding.

When Bover got into the thing and looked around, she realized she was *rich*. The thing was absolutely *stuffed* with machines. She had no idea what they did, but there were so many of them that she had no doubt at all that some of them, maybe *many* of them, would be as valuable as any heater or tunneler or anisokinetic punch.

The bubble burst when she found out she couldn't get back to Gateway. Her ship wouldn't move. No matter what she did to the controls it remained inert. It not only would not automatically return her to her port of origin, it wouldn't go anywhere at all.

Patricia Bover was stuck, some billions of miles from Earth.

As it turned out, the artifact was still operating; in a part of it that Pat Bover never saw, it was actually still producing food, half a million years after it was left there by the Heechee, out of the raw materials of the comets themselves—carbon, hydrogen, oxygen, and nitrogen, the basic elements that make up most of human diet and body. If Pat had known that—if she had forced herself to investigate the thing—she might have lived quite long while there. (Though not long enough for anyone to get there to rescue her, of course.)

She didn't know that, though. What she knew was that she was in serious trouble. What she did was send a long radio message to Earth, twenty-five light-days away, explaining where she was and what had happened. Then she got into her lander and launched it

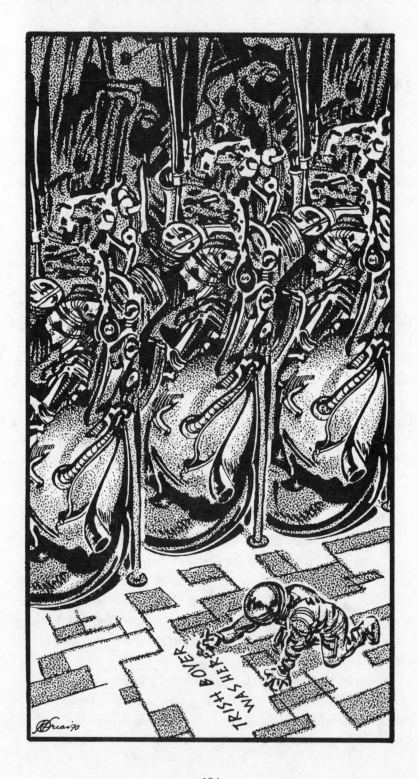

in the general direction of the Sun. She took a knockout pill and crawled into the freezer . . . and died there.

She knew the odds were against her. She wasn't properly frozen for any hope of revival, and anyway the chances were small that anyone would ever find her frozen body and try to revive it. And, as a matter of fact, no one ever did.

The Food Factory wasn't the only Heechee artifact in space which doubled as a trap for the unwary. There were altogether twenty-nine of these large objects—they were called "collection traps"—somewhere in the galaxy.

Patricia Bover's ill-fated find in the Oort cloud wasn't the only artifact the Heechee had left up and running. It wasn't even the only one to which a Gateway spaceship had a preprogrammed course. There was that other orbiting parking garage for spaceships that the Heechee had left around another star, far away—almost as big as Gateway; humans called it Gateway Two.

And then there was Ethel's Place.

Ethel's Place was discovered by an early one-woman mission. (The woman's name was Ethel Klock.) Then it was rediscovered by a group of Canadians in an armored Three; and re-rediscovered by another One, whose pilot was a man from Cork, Ireland, named Terrance Horran. The Canadians didn't just discover the artifact. They also discovered Ethel Klock, because she was there when they arrived. When Horran arrived he discovered them all, and later parties kept on discovering those who had come before, because they all stayed right there. As with Pat Bover on the Food Factory, it was a one-way destination for them all. There wasn't any return. The boards on all the ships nulled themselves on arrival.

They had no way of getting off the artifact.

That was a great pity in the minds of all of them, because Ethel's Place was a wonder. It was an object about the size of a cruise liner, but without any engines of any kind that they could discover. It had food machines, and air and water regenerators, and lights; and they were all still operating, even after all the millennia that had passed. The Heechee machines were built to last. Morever, there were a lot of astronomical instruments on Ethel's Place, and they were working, too.

The castaways had plenty of time to investigate their new home. They had nothing else to do. The food machines fed them; their lives were not threatened. They actually made quite a self-sufficient little colony. They might even have made it a permanent one, with generations of settlers coming along, if Klock had not been past the age of childbearing by the time the Canadians got there, or if the later arrivals had included any females.

They realized early that Ethel's Place was a kind of astronomical observatory.

What the observatory had been put there to observe was obvious at once. Ethel's Place was in orbit at a distance of about a thousand AU (which is to say, about five light-days) from a rather spectacular pair of astronomical objects. Binary stars weren't particularly interesting. This pair was unique. One of them was a fairly standard kind of star, though a rarish one—a hot, pulsating, super-giant specimen of the young and violent class called type F. That by itself would have been worth a little bonus money—if they had had any way of reporting it—but its companion was a lot stranger. The type-F star had a tilted ring of hot gas around it, suggesting that it was still in the process of reaching its final stage of starhood. The companion was *all* gas, and not very hot gas, at that—an immense, nearly transparent disk of the stuff.

The more they looked at it, the stranger it got. Stars were supposed to be *spheres*. They weren't supposed to be *disks*. The disk-shaped companion was hard to observe anyway, even with Heechee optics. Visually, it looked like nothing more than a faint scarlet stain on the sky. It was too cool to radiate much. The Heechee instruments couldn't tell them its temperature, because the Heechee had not been thoughtful enough to provide conversion tables into Celsius or Kelvin or even Fahrenheit scales. Klock's own best estimate was that it ran to maybe five hundred K—far cooler than the surface of Venus, for instance; cooler even than a log burning in a fireplace on Earth.

The best time to see it, they discovered, was when it was eclipsing the type-F companion star. Because the orbit of Ethel's Place was retrograde with respect to the disk, such eclipses happened more often than they would have if their artifact had somehow been stationary in the sky. They still did not happen *very* often. Ethel Klock had observed one eclipse alone, shortly after she landed. By the time of the next eclipse she had the Canadians and Horran to share the sight with, but that was more than twenty years later.

The story of Ethel's Place did finally have a happy ending for its captives—well, fairly happy. Ultimately human beings did learn how to make Heechee ships go where they wanted them to go. Shortly thereafter an exploring party in better command of its ship found the five castaways, and they were rescued at last.

It was a little late. By then Ethel Klock was in her seventy-eighth year, and even Horran was nearly fifty. They didn't even get their science bonuses, either. The Gateway Corporation had long since stopped issuing them, because the Gateway Corporation no longer existed.

They would have been out of luck anyway, they found, because even if they'd gotten back early they would not have collected much in the way of financial rewards. That binary star system was unfortunately not a new discovery. Indeed, it turned out to be a system that had been very familiar to astronomers on Earth, because of those very puzzling characteristics. The name of the star was Epsilon Aurigae, and its mysteries were no secret. They had been unlocked by human astronomers with conventional instruments when the binary's cool orbiting disk had passed between Earth and its type-F primary in the eclipse of the year A.D. 2000.

It was more than fifty years between the time the first Gateway prospector landed on one of those "collection traps" and the time the last of them was discovered. As many as eight separate missions might converge on one of them. When they did, they couldn't return. Most had food factories, either built in or supplied with shipments of food by automatic spacecraft from an independent factory nearby, so the castaways didn't starve, nor did they lack for water or air. A few did not have these amenities—not in working condition anymore, at least. In those cases all that was found were the abandoned Heechee ships and a few desiccated corpses.

Heecheeologists grew to believe that these "collection traps" served some purpose—maybe several purposes, though they could not be really sure what any of them were. None were accessible to planet dwellers; there were no tunnels on inhabited planets, nor were there any treasures where they could be reached without the use of spacecraft.

It seemed to be a sort of intelligence test posed by these vanished aliens. It was almost as though the Heechee, when they went to wherever they had gone, had deliberately left clues to themselves. But even the clues were hard to find. No intelligent race could find one until it had first mastered at least primitive interplanetary travel on its own.

And the greatest prizes were even more thoroughly concealed.

As a matter of record, it wasn't exactly a Gateway prospector who made the first *round-trip* expedition to the Food Factory. Pat Bover's was only one way. The expedition that made it possible for the Heechee carbon-hydrogen-oxygen-nitrogen (or "CHON") food to do something to help out hunger on Earth arrived there in an Earthly chemical rocket, spiraling out into the outer reaches of the solar system.

And they did more than that, because it was through the Food Factory that the second big discovery came along. It was called Heechee Heaven. It was the largest Heechee-made artifact ever discovered, more than half a mile long, twice the size of an ocean liner. It was shaped like a spindle (a familiar Heechee design), and it was not uninhabited. It held the descendants of the breeding group of australopithecines the Heechee had captured on Earth's surface, half

a million years before; it held one living human, the son of a pair of prospectors who had reached Heechee Heaven in their Gateway ship—and been trapped there. And it contained the stored minds (poorly stored, but the machines that did the job had never been designed for human beings; humans had not yet evolved when those machines were built) of more then twenty Gateway prospectors who had come there on one-way trips.

All that was wonderful . . .

It was more than wonderful, though. For the first time, Heechee technology was not only on hand but *accessible*. At last some of it could be understood . . . and copied . . . and even improved! Those treasures were not just satisfying scratches for the scientists' itch of curiosity, or wealth for a few lucky discoverers. They meant a better life for everyone.

And Heechee Heaven was not simply a space station. It was a *ship*. A vast one. A ship big enough to transport human colonists in quantities sizable enough to begin to make a dent in human misery—3,800 emigrants at a time, anywhere they chose to go—and keep on doing it, once a month, indefinitely.

And the colonization of the galaxy by the human race was possible at last.

PART EIGHT

LOOKING FOR COMPANY

The biggest "science" bonus the Gateway Corporation ever offered its prospectors wasn't really scientific. It was emotional. It proved that even the Gateway Corporation had some human feelings. The bonus was waiting there for any explorer who discovered a living, breathing Heechee, and it wasn't tiny. It came to fifty million dollars.

That was the kind of bonus any desperate Gateway explorer could dream about, but hardly any of them ever expected to claim it. Maybe the corporate masters didn't expect ever to pay it out, either. They all well knew that every sign of the Heechee anyone had ever found was hundreds of thousands of years old. They also suspected, very likely, that there might not be much chance that anyone who did discover a live Heechee would be allowed to come back and tell the human world what he had found.

But there were other bonuses in that same emotional area. They were lesser but still very worthwhile. The biggest one was the stand-

ing ten-million-dollar offer for the discovery of *any* intelligent race
of aliens. After a while, that was made a little easier. You could earn
it by finding any living aliens at all who showed the faintest signs
of smarts. You could even earn money for dead ones. There was a
flat million posted for the discoverer of the first *non*-Heechee artifact found, and half a million or so for the discovery of any one of
a variety of "signatures"—that is to say, of such unmistakable signs
of intelligence as a clearly coded radio transmission, or the detection
of synthetic gases in some planetary atmosphere somewhere.

It stood to reason, Gateway prospectors told each other as they
bought each other drinks in Gateway's Blue Hell, that it was just
about certain that somebody would find some of that kind of stuff
somewhere, sometime. They *had* to. Everyone knew that there *ought*
to be other intelligent races around. The Heechee couldn't possibly
be the *only* other intelligent beings in the universe. Could they?

That wasn't a new idea. As far back as the middle twentieth
century scientists had been listening for signals from other civilizations in space and trying to calculate the probability of ever hearing
one. A fellow named Stephen Dole had calculated that there ought
to be some 63,000,000 life-sustaining planets in the galaxy; later scientists, on tougher assumptions, cut the expected number down
much lower—but hardly any of them were willing to put it at zero.
Almost everybody agreed there ought to be *some*—and, in fact, Gateway prospectors did keep turning up planets where things did live.
And if there was life of any kind, it seemed a reasonable bet that
sooner or later some of that life would evolve toward intelligence . . .

But where were they?

Ultimately a couple of lucky breaks did begin to turn up a few
such interesting discoveries, though they were very sparse and slow
in coming.

The first definite *signs* of an alien intelligence (not counting the
Heechee themselves, of course) were detected by a three-person crew

from Pasadena, California, Earth. They came out of faster-than-light drive in orbit around a promising-looking sun (it was identified as a G-4, pretty close to Earth's own primary in type and suitability), and discovered quickly that there was a good-sized planet right in the middle of the habitability zone.

The trouble was, the planet was a mess. Most of one hemisphere was a patchwork of bare rock plains, punctuated with volcanoes, and the thing was *hot*. It didn't have much in the way of oceans. It didn't even have anything like as much of an atmosphere as its mass and constitution would have predicted.

However, what it did have was a dam. A big one.

The dam was on the less ruined side of the planet. Even so, it was not at all in good shape. It wasn't a very high-tech dam, for that matter—half a kilometer of rock piled across a valley. It had once been a river valley, no doubt, but there was nothing left of the river at all. There wasn't much left of the dam, for that matter. But what there was could not have been natural. *Someone* had piled those rocks in that place for a definite purpose.

Martin Scranton and his two sisters tried to land on the planet. They made a landing, all right, but the heat sensors in their lander began to squawk warnings as soon as they touched down; the surface even around the dam was hotter than the boiling point of water. They did, they thought, see traces of what might have been other stone structures on a few mountaintops, but nothing in recognizable shape.

Back on the Gateway asteroid, the scientists decided that that planet had had some bad luck—bad enough to be struck by some wandering body, probably something the size of Callisto; the impact had boiled off the seas, buried much of the planet under molten rock, driven the atmosphere into space—and, oh, yes, certainly, killed every organic thing that had ever inhabited it.

So Scranton hadn't found intelligent life. He did claim that he had at least found a place where intelligent life had once been. The Gateway Corporation couldn't call it a success, in terms of the discovery bonus offered. But still . . .

They took a long time to think it over, then paid half the bonus for a good try.

The first *living* nonhuman intelligent race the human explorers found didn't count. They weren't all *that* nonhuman, and they weren't all that intelligent, either. (For that matter, they weren't even discovered by a Gateway ship; the people who found them were moping around the extremes of Earth's own solar system in a primitive Earth-designed rocket ship.) What these particular "aliens" were were the remote descendants of a tribe of Earthly australopithecines, and the place they were found was on the big Heechee ship (or artifact), orbiting out in Sol's Oort cloud of comets, called "Heechee Heaven."

Of course, as we have seen, those old australopithecines hadn't gotten there by themselves. The Heechee had taken them away for breeding stock, in that long-ago visit to prehuman Earth. Then they had left them to the care of machine nursemaids—for half a million years and more.

The second race of aliens was better. It took a long time before they were found, but they were clearly the real thing at last. They were *definitely* intelligent—they proved it by traveling through interstellar space on their own! But they were a bit of a disappointment, all the same. They certainly weren't much fun to talk to.

They weren't exactly found by a Gateway prospector, either—the whole Gateway Corporation was pretty nearly history by the time these folks got discovered. It still existed, of course. But Gateway no longer was where the action was, for by then human beings had learned to copy a lot of Heechee technology and were venturing into new areas of the galaxy on their own.

At that point, one interstellar ship, on what had become a fairly routine cruise, detected an unfamiliar vessel. It turned out to be a photon-sail ship, slowly chugging along between stars on a voyage of centuries.

That certainly was not Heechee technology! Nor was it human, not even australopithecine: the long-awaited truly alien race had at last been located!

But actually they had been discovered quite a while earlier, it turned out—by the Heechee themselves, in fact. The sailboat people were the descendants of what the Heechee had called the "Slow Swimmers" and human beings came to know as the "Sluggards." They were definitely alien, and definitely not Heechee, and definitely intelligent.

That was all they had to recommend them, though. The Sluggards were sludge dwellers. They lived in wandering arcologies in a semifrozen mush of methane and other gases, and, although they had really and truly managed to launch those photon-sail spaceships,

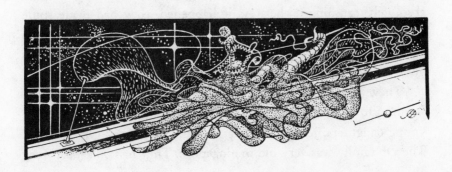

they didn't have many other attractive qualities. The worst thing was that they were terribly *slow*. Their metabolisms ran at the pace of free-radical reactions in the icy slush they lived in, and so did their thoughts, and their speech.

It took a long time before any human beings were able to establish any sort of useful communication with the snail's-pace Sluggards ... and by then, as it turned out, it didn't really matter.

MISSION *STINKPOT*

The four people on this mission spent a lot of time, and a lot of money, in court. What they were doing there was trying to win a suit against the Gateway Corporation for that ten-million-dollar bonus. They thought they had a pretty good case.

They didn't have a very good planet, though. Certainly it wasn't an attractive one. It was small and it was hot; its sun was a red dwarf, only a quarter of an AU away. And the planet really stank. That was what gave it its name.

The planet was also largely covered with water—not sparkling tropical seas but a sluggish ocean that bubbled methane into an atmosphere that was already mostly methane. You couldn't breathe the stuff. You wouldn't have wanted to if you could, because of the stink, and there was absolutely nothing of interest anywhere on the planet's few dry-land surfaces.

That wasn't good news for the people in the ship, but it wasn't absolutely crushing, either. As it happened, they had made some unusual preparations before they left Gateway, and thus they were equipped for more than the casual touchdown-and-lookaround of your average Gateway crew.

They were a family, and they came from Singapore. They were Jimmy Oh Kip Fwa, his wife Daisy Mek Tan Dah, and their two young daughters, Jenny Oh Sing Dut and Rosemary Oh Ting Lu. The Oh family was very old in Singapore. They had once been very rich, with a family fortune that had been made out of underwater mining. When Malaysia took the island over and expropriated all its industries the Ohs stopped being rich, but they had wisely socked away enough in Switzerland and Jakarta to finance their fares to Gateway, with enough left over to bring along some extra equipment. It was gear for underwater exploration. As Jimmy Oh told his family, "The Ohs made a lot of money out of sea-bottoms once. Maybe we can do it again."

Taking all that stuff with them meant that they could only fit four people in their Five, but then they didn't much want anyone else along anyway. And when they saw what sort of planet they had reached through the luck of the draw, Madame Mek was blessedly silent—at last—and their daughter Jenny said, "Jesus, Pop, you're not so dumb after all."

Even the Ohs hadn't brought along the kind of deep-sea diving gear and instrumentation that would let them make a systematic survey of Stinkpot's sea bottom. There was just too much sea bottom to explore, and too little time. What they had was half a dozen instrumented neutral-buoyancy balls. They dropped them into the global ocean at half a dozen randomly chosen points.

Then they went back to their orbiting ship and waited for transmissions.

As the buoys returned to the surface, the Ohs interrogated each one in turn about what it had found. That was disappointing. Of Heechee metal, the instruments had detected none at all. Of the kind of transuranic or other radioactive elements that might, just possibly, be worth mining and shipping back to Earth, also nothing.

But the instruments had picked up some electrical potentials that didn't seem to have any identifiable source. They were regular, in a pleasingly irregular kind of way. They made nice, rounded waves on a CRT, and when Jenny Oh, who had majored in cetacean ethology in school, slowed the signals down and played them through a sound synthesizer, they sounded . . . alive.

Were the signals language? If so, of what sort of living thing?

That was when the lawsuits started.

The Oh family said that language definitely proved the existence of intelligent life. The Corporation's lawyers said chirps and squeals weren't language, even if they did happen to be electromagnetic instead of acoustical. (Actually the signals did sound more like cricket chirps or bird calls than any articulate tongue.) The Ohs said how could crickets communicate by electrical impulses unless they were smart enough to build something like radio sets? The Corporation's lawyers said there wasn't any *radio* involved, just electric fields, and maybe the creatures had current-producing organs like an electric eel. The Ohs said, aha, then you admit you owe us at least the alien-life-discovery bonus, so pay it up right away. The Corporation's lawyers said, first show us your specimens. Or photographs. Or *anything* to prove these alien life forms are *real*.

Of course, all of this was in slow time. Each interchange in this dialogue took six or eight months of continuances and motion hearings and the taking of depositions. After three litigious years the Corporation grudgingly allowed a quarter-million-dollar settlement, which just about paid the Ohs' lawyer bills.

Then, years after that, someone else repeated their trip with better equipment. The new underwater probes had lights and cameras, and they found what was making the signals. It wasn't intelligence. It was worms—ten meters long, eyeless, living on the sulfurous exudation of undersea thermal vents. The things turned out on dissection to have electrical systems, just as the Ohs had claimed. That was all they did have that was of any interest at all.

Nevertheless, at least the Ohs were clearly entitled to another couple of hundred thousand, now that their discovery of life was confirmed. They didn't get it, though. They were no longer in any position to collect any further bonuses, having failed to return from their latest mission.

The intelligent-alien bonus didn't go entirely unclaimed, though. Two other parties of Gateway explorers did, in fact, collect their ten million apiece. They found what the Corporation, with some charity, agreed to call "intelligent" aliens.

Everyone admitted that the Corporation was stretching a point here. Even the lucky explorers did, though that didn't keep them from taking the money. The "Voodoo Pigs" looked like blue-skinned anteaters and wallowed in filth, like domesticated Earthly pigs. What made them "intelligent" was that they had developed an art form: they made little statuettes, nibbling them into shape with their teeth (well, the things they *used* for teeth), and that was more than any Earthly animal had ever done. So the Corporation philosophically paid off.

Then there were the "Quancies." They lived in the sea of a remote planet. They had tiny flippers, but no real hands; they weren't any good at manufacturing things for that reason, and so no one considered them technological. What they did have was a definite, and even a more or less translatable, language. They were definitely smarter than, say, dolphins or whales or anything else on Earth but man himself—and there, too, the Corporation paid its

bonus. (By then it was getting so rich that it was actually becoming generous, anyway.)

Those were all the live ones.

There were, to be sure, traces of other "civilizations" that were gone. A planet here and there had refined metal structures, not yet completely rusted away; others showed that somebody, sometime, had gone so far as to pollute its environment with certainly artificial radionuclides.

That was it.

And the more they found, the more the wonder grew. Where were the *old* civilizations? The ones who had reached Earth's stage of culture a million or a billion years before? Why hadn't they survived?

It was as though the first explorers into, say, the Amazon jungle had found huts, farms, villages, but instead of living denizens only corpses. The explorers would certainly wonder what had killed all the people off.

So wondered the Gateway prospectors. They could have accepted it if they had found no traces of any other intelligence (always, of course, not counting the Heechee themselves). Those members of the human race who cared about such things had been braced for that all along: the SETI searches and the cosmological estimates had prepared them for a lonely universe. But there *had been* other creatures that appeared to have been capable of as much technology and as much wisdom as the human race. They had existed, and now they were gone.

What had happened?

It was a long time before the human race found out the answer to that, and then they didn't like it at all.

PART NINE

THE AGE OF GOLD

While human beings were beginning to thread their way across the immensity of the galaxy, the world they had left behind was beginning to change. It took a long time, but at last the Heechee wonders the Gateway prospectors had brought home were beginning to make a real change for the better in the condition of the peoples of the Earth—even the poorest ones.

One key discovery unlocked all the rest. That was learning how to read the Heechee language. The hardest part of that was finding any Heechee language to read, because the Heechee did not seem to have been familiar with things like pencils, paper, or printing. It was a sure-thing bet in the opinion of everybody who ever gave it a thought that the Heechee must have had some way of recording things, but where was it?

When the answer turned up it was obvious enough: the long-mysterious "prayer fans" were actually Heechee "books." That is, it was obvious after the fact—though the tricky bit was that the things couldn't be read without some high-tech aid.

Once the records were identified as records, the rest was up to linguists. It wasn't all that hard. It certainly was no harder, say, than the long-ago decipherment of "Linear B," and it was made easier by the fact that places were discovered, on "Heechee Heaven" and elsewhere, where parallel texts could be found in both languages.

When the prayer fans were interpreted, some of the most intractable Heechee mysteries became crystal clear. Not the least of them was how to reproduce the Heechee faster-than-light drive. Then colonization could really begin. The great ship that had been called "Heechee Heaven" was the first to be used for that purpose, because it was already there. It ferried thousands of poverty-stricken emigrants at a time to new homes on places like Peggy's Planet, and that was only the beginning. Within five years that ship was joined by others, now human made—just as fast; even bigger.

And on the home planet itself . . .

On the home planet itself, it was the CHON-food factories that made the first big difference.

Simply put, what they did was end human starvation forever. The Heechee's own CHON-food factories orbited in cometary space—that was the reason for the long-baffling Heechee fascination with Oort clouds, now answered at last. The human-made copies of

these factories could be sited anywhere—that is, anywhere there was a supply of the basic four elements. The only other raw material they needed was enough of a salting of impurities to fill out the dietary needs.

So before long the CHON-food factories sat on the shores of the Great Lakes in North America and Lake Victoria in Africa and everywhere else where water and the four elements were present and people wanted to eat. They were along the beaches of every sea. No one starved anymore.

No one died of hunger before his time—and before long it was almost true that no one died at all. This was for two reasons. The first of them had to do with surgery, and, peculiarly, with the CHON-food factories, as well.

For a long time human beings had known how to substitute transplants for any worn-out organ. Now the replacement parts no longer had to be butchered out of cadavers. The same system that made CHON-food, considerably refined, could be induced to man-

ufacture tailor-made human organs to implant into people in need. (A whole wicked industry of assassinations for the marketplace collapsed overnight.) Nobody had to die because a heart, lung, kidney,

bowel, or bladder wore out. You just turned over your specifica-
tions to the people at the spare-parts division of the CHON-food
factory, and when they pulled your new organs out of their amni-
otic soup the surgeons popped them in place.

In fact, all the life sciences flowered. The Heechee food factories
made it possible to identify, and then to reproduce or even create,
a thousand new biological agents—anti-antigens; antivirals; selective
enzymes; cell replacements. Disease simply passed out of fashion.
Even such long-endured traumas as tooth decay, childbirth, and the
common cold became history. (Why should any woman suffer
through parturition when some other breeding machine—say, a
cow—could be persuaded to accept the fertilized ovum, nurture it
to ripeness, and deliver it healthy and squalling?)

And then there was the second reason. If, in spite of everything,
a person did finally die of simple overall decay, he didn't have to
die *completely*.

At least, there was another Heechee invention—it had been first found on the ship called "Heechee Heaven"—that robbed death of some of its sting. The Heechee's techniques for capturing a dead person's mind in machine storage produced the "dead men" on Heechee Heaven. Later, on Earth, it produced the enterprise called "HereAfter, Inc.," the worldwide chain of operators that would take your deceased mother or spouse or friend, put his or her memory into computer space, and permit you to converse with him or her whenever you liked—forever. Or as long as someone paid the storage charges for his or her datafile.

At first that certainly wasn't quite the same as being really alive. But it was a whole lot better than being irrecoverably dead.

Of course, as the technology matured (and it matured very fast), machine storage of human intelligence got easier and a great deal better.

When it got really good it began to raise some unexpected problems. Surprisingly, the problems were theological. The promises of Earthly religions were being fulfilled in a way the religious leaders had never planned, for indeed it seemed now to be true that "life" was only a sort of overture, and that "death" was in fact nothing more than the stepping stone to "eternal bliss in Heaven."

The dying man who then woke up to find himself no more than a collection of bits in the datafile of the immense computer networks might well wonder why he had clung to life in his organic body so long, for the machine afterlife had everything going for it. He had lost nothing through death. He still could "feel." The machine-stored ate as much as they liked—neither cost nor season were factors in planning a menu—and if they chose they excreted, too. (It did not matter that the "food" the "dead man" ate was only symbolically represented by bits of data, because so was he. He could not tell the difference.) All the biological functions were possible. He was deprived of none of the pleasures of the flesh. He could even make love with his dearest—provided only that she had stored herself in the same net—or with any number of dearests, real and imaginary, if that was how his tastes went. If he wanted the society of the still-living friends he had left behind, there was nothing to stop him representing himself to them (as a machine-generated hologram) in order to have a conversation, or a friendly game of cards.

There was also travel; and, perhaps most popular of all, there was work.

After all, the basic human work is only a kind of date processing. Humans don't dig the foundations for skyscrapers. Machines do that; all the humans do is run the machines, and that could be done as readily from machine storage as in the flesh.

All those books that the deceased had been meaning to read—the plays, the operas, the ballets, the orchestral performances—now there was time to enjoy them. As much time as he chose. Whenever he chose.

That was heaven indeed. The dead person's style of life was

exactly what he wanted it to be. He didn't have to worry about what he could "afford" or what was "bad for him." The only limit was his own desire. If he wished to be cruising in the Aegean or sipping cold rum drinks on a tropical beach, he only had to order it. Then the datastores would summon up any surround he liked, as detailed as any reality could be and just as rewarding. It was almost like living in a perfect video game. The operative word is

"perfect," for the simulations were just as good as the reality; in fact they were *better*: Tahiti without mosquitoes, French cuisine without gaining weight, the pleasure in the risks of mountain-climbing without the penalty of being killed in an accident. The deceased could ski, swim, feast, indulge in any pleasure . . . and he never had a hangover.

Some people are never happy. There were a few of the formerly dead who weren't satisfied. Sipping aperitifs at the Café de la Paix or rafting down the Colorado River, they would take note of the taste of the Campari and the spray of the water and ask, "But is it *real?*"

Well, what is "real"? If a man whispers loving words to his sweetheart on the long-distance phone, what is it that she "really" hears? It isn't his own dear voice. That was a mere shaking of the atmosphere. It has been analyzed and graphed and converted into a string of digits; what is reconstituted in the phone at her ear is an entirely different shaking of the air. It is a simulation.

For that matter, what did she hear even when her darling's lips were only inches away? It was not her ear that "heard" the words. All the ear does is register changes in pressure by their action on the little stirrup and anvil bones. Just as all the eye does is respond to changes in light-sensitive chemicals. It is up to the nerves to report these things to the brain, but they only report coded symbols of the things, not the things themselves, for the nerves cannot carry the sound of a voice or the sight of Mont Blanc; all they transmit is impulses. They are no more real than the digitized voice of a person on a phone.

It is up to the mind that inhabits the brain to assemble these coded impulses into information, or pleasure, or beauty. And a mind that happens to be inhabiting machine storage can do that just as well.

So the pleasure, all the pleasures, were as "real" as pleasure ever is. And if the mere pursuit of pleasure began to pall, after a (subjective) millennium or two, he could *work.* Some of the greatest music of the period was composed by "ghosts," and from them came some of the greatest advances in scientific theory.

It was really surprising that, nevertheless, so many people still preferred to cling to their organic lives.

All of this led to a rather surprising situation, though it took awhile for anyone to realize it.

When the Gateway explorers started bringing back useful Hee-chee technology, the world population on Earth wasn't much more than ten billion. That was only a tiny fraction of all the human beings who had ever lived, of course. The best guess anybody would make about the total census was—oh, well, maybe—let's say, some-where around a hundred billion people.

That included everybody. It included you and your neighbor and your cousin's barber. It included the president of the United States and the pope and the woman who drove your school bus when you were nine; it included all the casualties in the Civil War, the American Revolution, and the Peloponnesian Wars, and their survivors, too; all the Romanovs and Hohenzollerns and Ptolemys, and all the Jukes and Kallikaks, as well; Jesus Christ, Caesar Augustus, and the innkeepers in Bethlehem; the first tribes to cross the land bridge from Siberia to the New World, and also the tribes who stayed behind; "Q" (an arbitrary name assigned to the unknown first man to make use of fire), "X" (the arbitrary name of his father), and the original African Eve. What it included was *everybody*, living or dead, who was taxonomically human and born before that first year of Gateway.

That came, as we said, to a grand total of 100,000,000,000 people (give or take quite a lot), of whom the great majority were deceased.

Then along came Heechee, or Heechee-inspired, medicine, and things got started.

The numbers of the living meat people doubled, and doubled again, and kept on doubling. And they lived longer, too. With modern medicine, they didn't die before they wanted to. With medical encouragement and no painful penalties, they generally had kids, and generally lots of them. And when they did "die" . . .

Well, when they did "die" they also still "lived" in mechanical storage, and among that growing electronic population there were no fatalities at all.

So the number of the living continued to increase, while the number of the truly dead remained essentially static, and the result was inevitable. But when the point was reached it still took everyone by surprise; for at last in human history the living outnumbered the dead.

All of that had some interesting consequences. The eighty-year-old woman writing her X-rated memoirs of youthful indiscretions couldn't drop the names of video stars, gangsters, and bishops anymore—not unless the indiscretions had really happened, anyway—because the video stars, gangsters, and bishops were still around to correct the record.

It was a great plus for the oldest persons in machine storage, though. The names that they dropped from their meat days were well and truly dead, and in no condition to dispute the stories.

It wasn't bad to be a meat person anymore. Hardly any of them were poor.

Well, they weren't *money* poor. Not even on Earth. Nor were they poor in possessions. All their factories with all their clever robots were turning out smart kitchen appliances and fun game machines and talk-anywhere video-telephones, and they were doing it all the time. The cities got really big. Detroit led the way in the old United States, with its three-hundred-story New Renaissance megastructures that covered everything from Wayne State University dormitories to the river; a hundred and seventy million people lived in that crystal ziggurat, and every one of them had personal TVs with three hundred channels and holographic VCRs to fill any gaps left by the networks. Out in the Navajo reservation the tribe (now eighty million strong) erected a more-than-Paolo-Soleri arcology; the lowest forty stories produced frozen diet meals, clothing, and woven rugs for the tourist trade, and all above was filled with extended Navajo families. On the sands of the Kalahari Desert, the

!Kungs entered a life of plenty and ease. China reached twenty billion that year, each family with its fridge and electric wok. Even in Moscow the shelves of the GUM department store were loaded with clock radios, playing cards, and leisure suits.

There wasn't any problem producing anything anyone wanted anymore. The energy was there; the raw materials cascaded down from space. Agriculture had become as rationalized as industry at last: robots planted the fields, and robots harvested the crops—genetically tailored crops, enriched with artificial nonpolluting fertilizers and trickle-irrigated, drop by drop, by smart, automatic valves. And the whole, of course, supplemented by the CHON-food factories.

And if anyone still felt that Earth was not giving him all he chose to desire—there was always the rest of the galaxy.

That was what the meat people had. What the machine-stored had, of course, was much more. It was *everything*. Everything they had ever wanted, and everything they could imagine.

Really, there was only one real problem with machine storage after death, and that was relative time.

That couldn't be helped. Machines move faster than meat. In the interactions between the machine-stored and the meat persons they had left behind, it was a considerable handicap to conversation. The machine-stored found the meat people desperately *boring*.

It was easy enough for the still-living to talk with their dear departed (because the dear departed hadn't really departed any farther than the nearest computer terminal), but it was not a lot of fun. It was as bad as trying to make small talk with the Sluggards all over again. While the flesh-and-blood person was struggling to complete a single question, his machine-stored "departed" had time to eat a (machine-stored) meal, play a few rounds of (simulated) golf, and "read" *War and Peace*.

The fact that the machine-stored moved so much faster brought about some emotional problems for their meat relicts, too. It was particularly disconcerting right after a death. By the time the funeral was over, and the bereft put in a call for the one who had gone before, the one who had gone on had likely gone to take a relaxing, if simulated, cruise through the (also simulated) Norwegian fjords, learned to play the (unreal) violin, and made a hundred new machine-stored friends. The survivors might still have tear stains on their cheeks, but the deceased had almost forgotten his dying.

In fact, when he thought about his life in the flesh his feelings were probably nostalgic, but also quite glad all that was over—like any elderly adult remembering his own blundering, confused, worried childhood.

As one small consequence, machine-storage put the undertakers out of business. The machine-stored did not need a mausoleum to be remembered. Deaths were still marked by ceremonies, but they were more like a wedding reception than a wake; the business went to caterers rather than funeral directors.

Psychologists worried about this for a while. With the dead still (sort of) alive, and even reachable, how would the bereaved manage their grief?

When push came to shove, the answer was obvious. Grief wasn't a problem. There wasn't much to grieve.

Unfortunately, full stomachs and comfortable lives do not necessarily make human beings good.

Such things probably do help, a little. Nevertheless, the worms of ambition and envy that live in the human mind are not easily sated. As far back as the twentieth century it was observed that the manual laborer who managed to promote himself from cold-water flat to a ranch house with a VCR and a sports car could still feel pangs of envy toward his neighbor with the jacuzzi and the thirty-two-foot cabin cruiser.

The human race didn't change just because they had acquired Heechee technology. There were still people who wanted what other people had badly enough to try to take it away from them.

So theft did not disappear. Nor did thwarted lovers, or brooding victims, or simple psychopaths who tried to heal their grievances by means of rape, assault, or murder.

An earlier age took care of such people either by caging them in penitentiaries (but the prisons turned out to be mere finishing schools for crime) or turning them over to the executioner (but was murder any less premeditated murder simply because it was the state that was doing it?).

The Age of Gold had better ways. They were less revengeful, and maybe less satisfying to some of the punishment-minded. But they *worked*. Society was at last fully protected from its renegades. If there were still prisons (and there were), they were manned by computer-driven robot guards who neither slept nor took bribes. Better than prisons, there were planets of exile, where severe offenders could be deported. A criminal dropped on a low-tech planet could probably feed himself and continue to live, but there was no way he could ever build himself an interstellar spaceship to get back to civilization.

And for the worst cases, there was HereAfter.

Their minds faithfully reproduced in machine storage, their bodies no longer mattered. They could be disposed of without a qualm. It was capital punishment without its depressingly *final* aspects. After the sentence was carried out, the criminals weren't dead. They were still alive—after a fashion, anyway—but they were rendered permanently harmless. From that sort of prison no one ever was paroled, and no one could ever manage to escape.

All it required in order to make all these things happen, given the knowledge of the devices themselves, was energy.

There, too, the Heechee came through. The secret of Heechee power generation came out of study of the core of the Food Factory; and it was cold fusion. It was the same compression of two atoms of hydrogen into one of helium that went on in the core of any star, but not at those same temperatures. The output heat of the reaction came at about 900 Celsius—a nearly ideal temperature for generating electricity—and the process was *safe*.

So the power was there. It was cheap. And it put ten thousand fuel-burning power plants out of business, so that the carbon-dioxide greenhouse warmup of the Earth came to a halt, and the pollution of Earth's air stopped overnight. Small vehicles burned hydrogen or ran by flywheel kinetic-energy storage. Everything else took its power off the grids.

Things were really getting to be very nice on Earth, because human technology hadn't stopped, either.

For not everything in mankind's flowering of science and technology was a gift from the Heechee. There were computers, for instance.

Human computers were intrinsically better and more advanced than those of the Heechee, because the Heechee had never gone the adding-machine-to-mainframe route. Their methods of dealing with data handling were quite different, and in some ways not as good. Once the human scientists had begun to figure ways of adding Heechee refinements to the already powerful human machines, there was an explosion of knowledge that sparked new technologies in every part of human life.

Quantum-effect devices had long since replaced the clumsy doped silicon microchips, and so computers had become orders of magnitude faster and better. No one had to tap out a program on a keypad any more. He told the computer what he wanted done, and the computer did it. If the instructions were inadequate, the computer asked the right questions to clear it up—it was face-to-face communication, a machine-generated hologram speaking to its flesh-and-blood master.

Heechee food and Heechee power ... human computers ... Heechee biochemistry allied to human medicine ...

The human world at last allowed true humanity to every person who lived on it. And if, even so, any human wanted more, there was a whole galaxy waiting for him that was now within his reach.

There remained the burning and never-forgotten question of the Heechee themselves.

They were elusive. Their works were everywhere, but no one had ever seen a living Heechee, though every last Gateway explorer had wanted to look, and almost every human on Earth dreamed (or had nightmares) of what they would be like when found.

Arguments raged. Answers were scarce. The prevailing theory was that somehow, in some tragic way, the Heechee had died off. Perhaps they had killed themselves in a catastrophic war. Perhaps they had, for reasons not known, emigrated to a distant galaxy.

Perhaps they had suffered a universal plague—or reverted to barbarism—or simply decided that they no longer wanted to bother with traveling through interstellar space.

What everyone agreed on, at last, was that the Heechee were *gone*.

And that was just where everyone was very wrong.

PART TEN

IN THE
CORE

It was not true that the Heechee had died. Certainly not as a race, and, funnily enough, in an astonishing number of cases they hadn't even died as individuals.

The Heechees were very much alive and well. The reason they were not found was simply that they didn't want to be. For good and sufficient reasons of their own, they had decided to conceal themselves from any unwelcome attention for a few hundred thousand years.

The place where the Heechee hid was in the core of the galaxy, within an immense black hole—a black hole so enormous that it contained thousands of stars and planets and satellites and asteroids, all orbiting together in a space so small that their combined mass had pulled space in around them. The Heechee were all there—several billion of them, living on some 350 roofed-over planets inside their Core.

To create their immense hidey-hole, the Heechee had tugged together 9,733 individual stars, together with their appurtenant planets and other orbiting objects. That gave them, among other things, some really spectacular nighttime skies. From the surface of the Earth, human beings can see at most maybe four thousand stars with the naked eye, ranging from fiery blue-white Sirius all the way down to the sixth-magnitude ones that lie on the squinting border of visibility. The Heechee had more than twice that many to look at, and they were easier to see because they were a whole hell of a lot closer—blue ones far brighter than that familiar Sirius, ruby ones almost as bright as Earth's Moon, asterisms of a hundred stars in a bunch and all wondrously bright.

Of course, that same stellar population density kept the Heechee from *having* much in the way of nights. Except when the clouds were thick they just weren't used to much darkness. On their planets inside the Core there was seldom a time when the collective stellar effulgence didn't give them light enough at least to read by.

With all those stars, they had plenty of planets to live on. The Heechee only occupied a fraction of the available planets, but they had made the ones they chose to live on very homey. Naturally, a

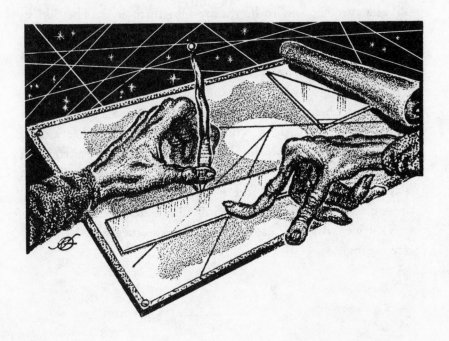

very high proportion of those planets were temperately warm, benign in atmosphere, and right-sized for the kind of surface gravity the Heechee enjoyed (not all that different from Earth's, as it happened). That wasn't any accident. They had naturally chosen the cream of the crop to shift into their Core colony so they could inhabit them. There they built their cities and their factories, and laid out their farms and cultivated their oceanic fish ponds—none of those things looked exactly like the human equivalents, but they all worked just as well. Generally they worked a lot better. All of this building and making and growing was so thriftily done that the Heechee avoided pollution and everything unsightly. They were as snug as bugs in a rug.

It wasn't quite perfect. But then, nothing is. Jamaica has hurricanes, Southern California has its Santa Ana winds, even Tahiti has its rainy seasons. The most nearly ideal of climates generally has a few unpleasant kinds of weather. The Heechee had their own weather problems in their Core hideaway. For them, it wasn't rain or wind, it was the built-in nastiness of any black hole. Black holes pull whatever happens to be nearby into themselves. They do so with great force, producing high velocities and a lot of turmoil. This expresses itself in radiation. It was only from this production of radiation that black holes were first detected by human astronomers, and it is deadly, ionizing stuff.

So everywhere in the Core there was a permanent shower of damaging charged particles, which meant that the Heechee usually had to roof over their worlds. The crystal spheres that surrounded every planet kept out the more dangerous radiation from all those nasty sources. Meanwhile, the Schwarzschild radius of their immense black hole kept out something they feared even more.

That was why they had retreated the way they had. Now they were waiting.

Of course, the Heechee needed a way in and out of their great black hole, and, of course, they had one. Human beings had the same thing, too, in some of those abandoned Heechee ships they had found, but it didn't do them much good because they didn't know they had it.

That was a general problem with Heechee technology. When human beings found pieces of it they also found a lot of confusion. The Heechee had not been kind enough to leave operating manuals for the humans to pore over. They hadn't even put labels on the machines—at least, not in any way that human beings could read. The best way for human beings to find out what all those gizmos and gadgets were for was what used to be called reverse engineering, which basically meant taking them apart to see how they worked.

The trouble with that was that when engineers tried it, the damned things often blew up. So they tended to treat the machinery with caution, and if they didn't know what it was for, and couldn't figure out any way of trying it out, they tended to leave it alone. Take that crystally, twisty rod sort of thing that was part of the furnishings of some, but not all, Heechee ships. They knew it had a purpose. They didn't know what it was.

If anyone on Earth had known where the Heechee lived, they might have guessed that one a lot sooner . . . but no one did, and so the human race had in its hands an instrument for penetrating black holes long before anyone knew what it could do.

It was a while before any human being knew exactly what a Heechee looked like, for that matter. Still, they are easy enough to describe.

A male Heechee is about five feet tall, on average. His head is the Aryan ideal Nordic squared-off block, only a little more so, though his skin color isn't Nordic at all. If he is male it is probably a sort of oak-bark brown; if female, she is generally somewhat paler. The Heechee skin looks as though it were carved out of shiny plastic. A dense, fine growth of hair covers his scalp, or would if he didn't keep it cropped very short. He smells ammoniacal to human beings—the Heechee themselves don't notice it. There is no iris to his eyes. There isn't really even a pupil, just a vaguely X-shaped dark blotch in the middle of a pinkish eyeball. His tongue is forked. And his general build . . .

Well, what you would think of a Heechee's bodily build would depend on whether you were looking at him from the front or from the side.

If a human being were squeezed flat, he would come out of it looking like a Heechee. Viewed from the front, your Heechee would look formidable; from the side (except for a rather potbellied, globular abdomen), quite frail. What he would most look like (though not so exaggerated) would be the cardboard-cutout skeletons children decorate their schoolrooms with at Halloween. This was especially true around the hip and leg joints, because the Heechee pelvis was structurally rather different from the human. The legs attached directly to the ends of the pelvis, like a crocodile's, so there was a considerable space between the legs as a Heechee stood erect.

The Heechee didn't waste that space. It was the most convenient place for a Heechee to carry anything, so the sorts of loads human beings would be likely to lug in their arms or on their shoulders the Heechee carried slung between their legs. In fact, all civilized Heechee carried a large, tapering pouch there. In it they kept two main items—the microwave generators they needed for their comfort, and the storage facilities for the "ancient ancestors" whose minds they carried around with them, as a human being might carry a pocket calculator—as well as their equivalents of fountain pens and credit cards and photos of their near and dear. And when the Heechee sat down, what they sat on was the pouch.

(Thus at one blow ended a half century of speculation on why the seats in the Heechee spacecraft were so user-unfriendly for human users.)

Although hard and shiny, the Heechee integument was not

thick. You could see the movement of the bones through it; you could even see the muscles and tendons working, especially when the Heechee was excited—it was a kind of body language, something like a human's grinding his teeth. Their speech was somewhat hissy. Their gestures were not at all like those of Earthmen. They didn't shake their heads in negation; they flapped their wrists instead.

The Heechee had descended from a race of burrowers like prairie dogs rather than arboreal tree climbers moved to the plains, as people had. Therefore the Heechee possessed several traits that their heredity had laid on them. No Heechee ever suffered from claustrophobia. They *liked* being in enclosed spaces. (That may have been why they enjoyed tunnels so much. It certainly was why they preferred to sleep in things like gunnysacks filled with wood shavings.)

Their family lives were not exactly like those of humans; nor were their occupations; nor were their equivalents of politics, fashion, and religion. They had two sexes, like people, and sex was sometimes obsessive in their minds—as with people—but for long periods they hardly thought about the subject. (Not very like most people at all.) Strangely, they had never evolved equivalents of such human institutions as a government bureaucracy (they hardly had a government) or a financial economy (they didn't even use money in any important sense). Humans didn't understand how they could operate without these things, but the Heechee thought that in those respects human ways were pretty repulsive, too. Since, by the time human beings got far enough out into space to have some chance of encountering Heechee, most employed human persons were in these "white-collar" occupations, they were startled to find that most Heechee were, in their view, unemployed.

It wasn't just that the human poli-sci and sociology professors wondered how the Heechee managed to get along without kings, presidents, or maximum leaders. Even on Earth, generations of anarchists, libertarians, and small-is-beautiful philosophers had been claiming that human beings didn't need such things, either. The real puzzle was how the Heechee had escaped having them anyway.

It took a number of anthropologists and cultural behaviorists a long time to come up with an explanatory theory. That phenomenon, too, seemed to have an evolutionary basis. It came from the fact that the pre-Heechee nonsapients—the primitive species they labeled "Heecheeids"—had burrowed in the ground like prairie dogs or trapdoor spiders. They did not form tribes. They staked out territories. Therefore Heecheeids did not conduct tribal wars or struggle for succession to a throne; there wasn't any throne to succeed to. No Heecheeid ever had any need or desire that conflicted with any other Heechee—as long as the other guy stayed out of his territory.

Of course, you can't build a high-tech, spacefaring civilization out of solitary, noninterfering individuals. But by the time the primitive Heechee had reached the point of projects so ambitious that they required the cooperation of many their habits were set. They had never formed the custom of patriotism. They didn't have nations to be patriotic to. They did have a code of behavior—"laws"—and institutions to codify and enforce them ("councils," "courts," "police"), but that was about it. Earthly governments spent most of their energies defending themselves against the attacks of—or waging their own attacks against—the governments of other nations. When the reciprocal threat was physical, the method of doing so was military. When the threat was economic, the effort was expressed in subsidies, tariffs, and embargoes. The Heechee didn't need such national enterprises, having no nations to compete with each other.

And so the Heechees lived in their crowded Core, contentedly enough, while they waited to be discovered.

Their lives within the Core were not entirely normal by human standards, however.

There was one significant divergence from normality. The Heechee had been living there for some half a million years—since not long after they visited the early Earth and carried away a handful

of australopithecines to see what the stupid little beasts might de-velop into, given a chance—but it didn't seem that long to them.

Albert Einstein would have immediately understood why that was. In fact, he had predicted something like it. The Heechee were within a black hole. Therefore they obeyed the cosmological rules governing black holes, including the phenomenon of time dilation. Time that sped along in the outer galaxy passed with glacial slow-ness inside the Core; the ratio was something like 40,000 to 1. That was a very great difference—so great that many of the Heechees who had left their ships on Gateway were still alive inside the Core. Oh, they had grown a bit older, yes. Time hadn't stopped. But for them only a few decades had passed, not half a million years.

And when the Heechee ran away and hid they left sentinels behind them. They had a plan.

There was an unfortunate element of risk to their plan. The Heechee could not be certain that some other intelligent, spacefaring race would evolve and find the artifacts they had left and use them; and if those things didn't happen, the plan was wasted. Still, that was the way to bet it. They counted on it, in fact; and so the Hee-chee had set robot sentinels in concealed places in the galaxy to find these new races when they showed up.

KELLY FREAS.

When the human race began to make noise in the galaxy, the Heechee's watchmen heard it.

The Heechee then employed that twisted crystal and ebon rod that they called the Heechee equivalent of "can opener" to come out and check their "collection traps," to see just what had begun to happen in the galaxy in the last few centuries (or, from their viewpoint, couple of days). As a normal precaution, the Heechee sent a routine scouting party out to investigate . . .

But that is, really, quite another story.

ABOUT THE AUTHOR

Frederik Pohl has been everything one man can be in the world of science fiction: fan (founder of the fabled Futurians), book and magazine editor, agent, and, above all, writer. As editor of *Galaxy* in the 1950s, he helped set the tone for a decade of sf—including his own memorable stories such as *The Space Merchants* (in collaboration with Cyril Kornbluth).

He has also written *The Way the Future Was*, a memoir of his first forty-five years in science fiction. Frederik Pohl was born in Brooklyn, New York, in 1919, and now lives in Palatine, Illinois.